THE CURSE OF ASH AND BLOOD

LOU WILHAM

Midnight Tide
PUBLISHING

 Created with Vellum

ALSO BY LOU WILHAM

The Curse Collection
    The Curse of The Black Cat
    The Curse of Ash and Blood
    The Curse of Flour and Feeling

The Sea Witch Trilogy
    Tales of the Sea Witch
    Tales of the Littlest Mermaid

The Clockwork Chronicles
    The Girl in the Clockwork Tower
    The Unicorn and the Clockwork Quest

Villainous Heroics
    Villainous

The Heir To Moondust
    The Prince of Starlight
    The Prince of Daybreak

THE CURSE OF
ASH & BLOOD

LOU WILHAM

PROLOGUE

In a small fishing village—so small in fact, it boasted no name—on the coast of the Black Sea, there was once a young mage with two different colored eyes, one blue and one green, and a face full of freckles. His mother had named him Fable before she passed on, leaving him in the care of his grandfather. With a clever mind and a shy smile, Fable took his duties as the village's mage very seriously. He spent his days tending to his fellow villagers and their animals, and his evenings practicing his art or dabbling in swordplay.

Near that village lived a ferocious, volatile dragon who had never been given a name. Blaze is what he went by— when he could be bothered to deal with others—and he hated everyone, indiscriminately.

ONE

When the first blow hit the tiny village, it rumbled low through Fable's booted feet, drawing his attention away from the vials in his hands. Wide, two-toned eyes flicked up to gaze out the window, and narrow on a billow of smoke drifting above the low rooftops surrounding his home.

"What the hell was that?" Grandfather asked, emerging from the small bedroom at the rear of their cottage. One gnarled hand scrubbed at his face as he groaned and squeezed bright blue eyes shut. "Can't an old man take a mid-afternoon nap in peace anymore?"

Another blow rocked the earth—this time close enough to topple Grandfather. Fable rushed to steady him. "I'll see what's going on," he grunted. "You stay here."

With the leather bag of potions slung over his shoulder, Fable raced out onto the dirt street, heading straight for the smoke. Another blow nearly knocked him off his feet, but he crouched low to maintain his balance and ran faster. Whatever danger lurked ahead was growing more destructive by the minute.

Fable lifted a freckled hand to brush curly brown hair back from his eyes and survey the scene. What awaited him on the outskirts of the village was utter chaos. Smoke rose from a flaming fishing boat, a woman ran past him screaming at the top of her lungs, and right in the center of it all—peeking through the smoking air—was a flutter of thin red wings above the rooftops of the surrounding homes.

"The dragon," Fable whispered to himself in awe, body stilling for a moment as the smoke cleared to reveal the deadly glint of the beast's eyes. The dragon had lived in the caves overlooking their village for as long as Fable could remember, but had never once bothered with them. It seemed—to Fable, at least—that the creature was no threat to them, or it hadn't been. Already reaching for the sword at his side, he rushed forward, prepared to help detain the beast, or at least keep it from destroying the village any further.

A small group of men from the village, who prided themselves on their skills as warriors, were backing the dragon slowly the way it had come with drawn swords. When he reached them, their leader—a brash thug named Jacop—turned to eye him narrowly. "Get back, Fable. This fight isn't for mages. Leave this work to the men!" He sneered over his shoulder before shoving Fable aside.

"I can help," Fable protested, grabbing the man to tug him out of the way as the dragon swung its great red tail in their direction. "I can put it to sleep," he muttered. With one hand still holding up his sword defensively, he dug through the satchel at his side with the other. His fingers slipped over glass bottles and vials—recognizing them each by shape and the texture of the glass—in search of the brilliant purple sleeping draught.

"Put it to sleep?" another snorted, lunging towards the

dragon to slice at its swinging tail. The beast roared in pain. "We want to kill it!"

"Kill it?" Fable asked, dark brows knitting. No, that couldn't be right. That would — "We can't kill it! It's a bloody dragon! What do you want to do? Start a war?" he shouted over the continued pained roar from the creature. "It'll raze this entire damn country if we try to kill it!"

"Well, we ain't gonna give it the chance. Are we boys?" Jacop shouted arrogantly, and the others joined in.

A snort drew their attention up, up, up, and Fable's mismatched eyes met narrowed amber eyes set in a face of red scales. The creature was watching them, and if Fable didn't know any better, he'd think it looked amused. "Idiots," it scoffed. All the men blinked up at it in confusion. "I'll see you around, little mage." Its reptilian mouth twitched into a smirk, wings spreading wide, and it took flight, leaving the group of men coughing up dust.

GRANDFATHER WAS SITTING at the table waiting for him when Fable slammed the door hard enough to shake their small home. A scowl marred his freckled features, and his brows knit together in frustration. *Those fools. They ought to know better! When would people learn? Violence would only beget more violence.*

"Well?" Grandfather asked, drawing Fable from his thoughts. The old man looked twenty years older as he tapped blunt nails against the wooden table to dispel some of his anxiety. "What was it?"

"The dragon," Fable murmured tiredly, sliding his satchel onto the table before flopping into the chair opposite Grandfather. "The warriors," he grumbled sarcastically, rolling his mismatched eyes. "Want to head into the hills in a few days to kill it."

Grandfather scoffed. "They'll be slaughtered, and then what?"

"And then it'll come back to finish the job on the village," Fable answered, not even having to second guess what would come next. He may not have seen it firsthand, but everyone knew what dragons were like. They were vengeful, ferocious creatures, and when possible, it was best to leave them alone. "It won't stop until everything is on fire, and we're all dead."

"Exactly," Grandfather agreed with a somber nod. "I told everyone to leave that beast alone. It's been living in the hills since you were born, and never bothered with any of us." Grandfather was a sensible man, so of course, he had offered a sensible solution to the dragon—leave it alone and it would leave them alone. Unfortunately, it seemed he'd either been mistaken—Fable doubted that—or someone had disturbed the beast.

Fable sighed, head falling to the table with a soft *thunk*. "What're we going to do?"

"Hmm..." Grandfather hummed thoughtfully, scratching at the soft blond stubble on his chin. He was silent for a few minutes as he thoroughly considered their options. When his voice returned, it was soft and calm, but determined. "Perhaps it's time the council held a village meeting about this problem. Seems the only way to keep glory hounds out of the mountains might be to make it law."

"You think that'll help?" Fable asked doubtfully, not lifting his head from where his face was smashed against the table.

"Certainly can't hurt."

THE VILLAGE HALL—WHICH also happened to be the schoolhouse, a courthouse, and a meeting room for a knitting circle—was loud. Fable's ears rang with a hundred shouts as everyone from the village tried in vain to be heard over everyone else. He knew better than to add his voice to the fray; it wouldn't do him any good. Instead, he waited, green and blue eyes flicking around the angry faces that filled the room.

"That is enough," came the booming voice of the head elder as he slammed his walking stick into the wooden floorboards, silencing the crowd. Once everyone had settled, his grey eyes swept the room. Grandfather Ceylon was a stern man who would not take kindly to any foolishness. "Grandfather Alperen has brought it to my attention that while he has advised against bothering the dragon in the past, he overheard some young men in the village discussing their plans to head into the mountains a week ago. They wished to find victory in slaying the beast, and he warned them away from such an action. Is this true?"

Unease settled through the crowd. People shifted from foot to foot, including the men standing beside Fable—who had run in, swords drawn, to kill the poor creature. No one stepped up to answer the question.

"Since no one seems brave enough to step forward now —perhaps I am more frightening than a dragon—I will continue. From this day forth, no child of this village shall seek such nonsensical pursuits. Our children will not go on quests and play knight in search of notoriety." The words seemed to echo throughout the silent hall.

"Then what will we do about the dragon?" someone

from the back shouted, but they dared not step forward to reveal their face.

"It will come back!" another voice shouted in agreement. The room erupted in a chorus of nervous chatter again.

"We have to kill it before it kills us," Jacop snarled, already drawing his sword as if to slay the beast right then and there. Murmurs of agreement replaced the panic. "Let me take my men up there; we'll bring back its head on a pike!"

"No!" Fable shouted, almost before he'd even thought the word. Everyone turned to him, shock and judgement in their eyes. Insecurity washed over Fable, but he swallowed it down. "All that will do is invite war with the creature, and then what happens when you fail?"

"I won't fail," the man snorted, rolling his eyes.

Fable's expression hardened, his fists tightening at his sides. "You will, and when you do, you'll leave the entire village vulnerable for your arrogance."

Jacop growled, closing the distance between him and Fable. The larger man grabbed Fable by his collar and lifted him up. His other arm pulled back as if to strike the young mage. Fable had just enough time to throw his hands up, hoping to protect his face. "You little—" Jacop snarled viciously.

"Enough!" Grandfather Ceylon shouted, stilling all motion throughout the hall. "Jacop, let go of the boy." Fable's boots settled back to the floor, but his heart was still pounding in his ears. "Speak, Fable."

With a deep breath, Fable tried to calm his racing thoughts. He tucked his hands into his pockets to keep from picking uselessly at his nails. "When they," he started, but it came more like a squeak than words, so he inhaled again before starting over. "Before the dragon left, he spoke to us. It seems he's intelligent and thus we can reason with him."

He could almost hear the collective blink of disbelief from the surrounding people. His ears reddened in embarrassment, feeling every eye in the room on him. "You want to... reason with a dragon?" Grandfather Ceylon asked incredulously.

"Yes," he began, swallowing roughly as heat crawled up his neck. "Yes, sir. I want to reason with the dragon."

"And should this plan also fail?"

"The sweet little mage will be an afternoon snack!" Jacop laughed loudly, followed by chortles from the friends that surrounded him.

Fable bit his lip, lifted his chin, and met Jacop dead on with his mismatched eyes. "I'll use magic to subdue him," he insisted earnestly. "Not everything must be solved by bloodshed."

"You don't have enough magic in your scrawny body to tame a mouse, much less subdue a dragon," Jacop jeered, his face split in a malicious smile.

Fable's Grandfather pressed a hand to his shoulder to keep the young mage from flying off the handle, as Fable's fists tightened at his sides again. "Should he fail, we will ask the witch for help," Grandfather offered reasonably.

There was a moment—hardly the length of a heartbeat—where Fable was sure that the elders would laugh in his face and tell him 'no.' Instead, they all nodded in agreement. "Very well, Fable. We will try it your way, but if you fail the dragon will need to be slain lest it attack the village in revenge. And you and your Grandfather will no longer be welcome here. You will be exiled," Grandfather Ceylon said seriously.

The gravity of his words sunk into Fable's stomach, but he stuttered out a weak, "Yes—Yes, sir."

THE RIDE into the mountains was uneventful. A journey that Fable had planned to take him till sunset only took about half the day, leaving him little time to dwell on what he was about to do. Although he had put on a brave face before the elders, and the other villagers, he was terrified. He pulled his horse to a stop before the caves, before turning to take one last look at his home below. Doubt coated his palms and the back of his neck in a thin sheen of sweat. "This might be goodbye," he whispered to the horse as there was no one else to listen. "I might not come back from this." He'd hardly thought the words till now, but they slipped from his tongue with ease.

The horse—in all its infinite wisdom—pressed its muzzle to Fable's cheek. Without so much as a neigh in response, it nudged the boy lightly.

"Yes, I suppose you're right," Fable said with a nod. "May as well get it over with." He squeezed his eyes shut, trying to commit the sight of his home to memory, and then turned to head into the darkness of the cave. "Hello?" he called, the sound echoing back to him. "Mister Dragon?"

Nothing. Only the sound of his words echoing in the emptiness greeted him. Something crunched beneath his feet, and it took everything Fable had not to look down to find out what creature's bones he'd stepped on—he prayed it hadn't been a human. Still, he steeled himself and wandered in further. The smell of sulfur choked him a moment before the soft footfalls of another echoed around him.

"Didn't anyone ever tell you it is rude to come into a person's home without being invited?" a soft, harsh voice reverberated off the walls in a tsk. "Naughty, naughty, little mage. Where are your manners?"

"I, um..." Fable swallowed roughly, his eyes narrowing to see through the gloom of the cave to whoever was speaking. "I'm sorry?"

"Was that a question or an apology?" A strange human-shaped figure walked closer, its head tilted in curiosity.

"Both?" Fable frowned at his own words. *Stupid, Fable,* he chided himself.

A soft snort left the figure, and he stepped into the light cast from the mouth of the cave. The speaker was a slender boy with strawberry blond hair and pale features. Stumbling backward in shock, Fable tripped over a bone and fell onto his backside with a thud. Another snort of laughter filled the air. "You humans are all so clumsy, aren't you?" the boy asked condescendingly.

"Where's the dragon?" Fable asked, pulling himself to his feet. He tried to make sense of what he was seeing. This was the dragon's cave, was it not? Why was a human boy living in it?

One blond brow quirked, and the boy bowed low before lifting glinting amber eyes to meet Fable's gaze. Fable had but a moment to see the similarity, and to take notice of the long thin scar that ran down the side of the boy's face. "Blaze, if you please. Did you come here to kill me, little mage? That's what your friends came to do. They wanted to kill me and take my scales back to the village like a trophy." A snarl left the dragon's lips as he bared sharp incisors at Fable. "It nearly worked. They gave me this." His finger glided down the scar that ran from temple to cheek on the side of his face.

"I-I-I didn't. I didn't come here to-to kill you," Fable stuttered, already backing towards the entrance in panic.

"Then what?" Blaze shouted, the sound causing the walls to shake.

Fable grappled for something, anything to put space between them. Instead of a bone, or a rock, or even sure footing, what Fable found was his sword. He swung it forward, his hand shaking as he pointed the tip at the boy. "I just—"

"Wanted to lop off a piece of me and take it home to your mommy!" Blaze roared, eyes glowing in his rage as a set of large red wings sprouted from his back. "Well, I'll show you, stupid human!"

Fable stumbled again, losing his footing. Awe stilled his movements as the boy shifted into the great red beast that had terrorized his village not but two days prior. How could something so beautiful be so deadly? Maybe that was simply the nature of beautiful things.

"I just want—" Fable started, but the dragon charged at him, leaving Fable no time to explain. On instinct, he reached into his satchel and pulled out a glass bottle. It smashed against the ground, enveloping the cave in thick purple smoke. With his cowl over his mouth to keep from breathing in the sleeping draught, Fable took off in a run. He leaped onto his horse, nudging it into an all-out gallop. "We have to see Gwydion before he wakes up," he rasped, steering the horse towards the tiny hut on the outskirts of the village. The witch would know what to do.

BY THE TIME Fable reached Gwydion's hut, he and his horse were both covered in a thick layer of sweat and the sun was sinking below the horizon. A quick glance over his shoulder told him that the dragon hadn't followed—yet. "That won't keep him out very long," Fable muttered to himself. "It would keep a human out for days—but a dragon? No, with the added bodyweight, and magic, I'll be lucky if he's not already tracking me."

"What's with all the racket out here?" a smooth, deep voice asked as a red head peeked out of the door, beads jangling around their neck.

"Sorry to bother you, sir." Fable blinked at the figure for a moment. He drank in the long flowing scarves, the obscene amount of jewelry, the long red braid of hair, and the kohl-rimmed eyes, and amended, "Madam?"

"Gwydion will suffice," the witch responded with a kind smile. "Now, come in, boy. Before you let in the bugs."

"Uh, yes, Gwydion." Fable slid off his horse and made his way inside, but not before glancing nervously at the caves atop the mountain—no dragon, yet. Once inside, Gwydion ushered him into a large chair. "I don't really have time for — " Fable tried to argue, but the witch deposited a cup of tea into his hands without preamble. There was a pot made up and two cups sitting on a serving tray as if Gwydion had been expecting company. "That's sweet of you, but I really don't have time—"

"Drink," Gwydion instructed, refusing to say anything else until Fable had taken a careful sip. With a nod, Gwydion sat back in their own chair. "Now, tell Auntie Gwydion why you're here, hmm?"

"I've come to ask for help to tame the dragon," Fable spoke plainly. He had no such time for flowery language or explanations, the dragon would be on his tail soon enough.

"Why?" Keen, golden eyes—nearly hidden behind layers of expensive-looking silk—narrowed on Fable.

"To protect my village, and to protect him. If I can't do anything about him, the village elders want to send a small army into the mountains to slay him." Fable's words were soft. He had thought little about the notion to protect a dragon, nor how foolish it might sound. Now—saying the words out loud—they sounded rather silly. Insane, almost. Dragons were beasts of immense power, what need did one have of a little mage's protection?

"Why?" Gwydion pressed again. Fable blinked up at the witch in confusion, meeting the witch's eyes for the first time. "By land and by sky," Gwydion whispered thoughtfully, head tilting as they stared into the boy's eyes.

"W-what?" Fable frowned.

"Why do you want to protect the dragon?" Gwydion clarified, acting as if they'd said nothing else.

"Oh, uh, that." Fable shifted in his seat, eyes blinking down at his tea for a moment. He'd half expected Gwydion to laugh in his face, but now he needed to put words to the emotions swelling within himself. "I don't think we should kill magical creatures if we don't have to." He shrugged. Gods, he was an idiot.

"Hmm..." the witch hummed thoughtfully. "Well, I'm afraid I can't help you."

"What?" Fable's head jerked up, frowning deeply. "What do you mean you can't help me?"

Gwydion took his teacup and made to escort him to the door. "Precisely, as I said—I can't help you. Magic does not tame dragons."

"Then what does?" Fable sputtered, doing his best to dig his heels into the wood floor, but the witch was surprisingly strong. "If magic can't tame a magical creature, what can?"

Gwydion gave no answer and had almost shoved the

boy to the door when they heard the flapping of wings, and a hard wind blew open the hut's windows. "Damn it," Gwydion grumbled under their breath.

Fable didn't think, he acted. He lunged outside; sword drawn. "Leave the witch alone, your quarrel is with me!" his shout echoed off the trees, as he tucked Gwydion behind his back.

Blaze reared back, opening his broad mouth and shooting a burst of fire towards them. Fable grabbed Gwydion around the waist and ducked them both out of the way in time, but the flame caught the little hut, and in moments half of it was a husk of cinders.

"My house!" Gwydion screeched.

Neither the dragon nor the mage seemed to notice as they circled one another. Blaze lashed out with a massive claw, and Fable sprang back to counter with his sword. Another circle, another round of flames, and the other half of the little hut was reduced to ash.

"My wardrobe!" Gwydion shrieked, running towards the smoldering building to salvage some of their things.

Fable spun, grabbing for Gwydion's clothes to stop them. "You can't go in there! You'll—"

In his distraction, one broad swing of the dragon's tail sent the boy flying. Fable's head knocked hard against a tree. He felt more than saw the trickle of blood from the wound on the back of his head as it coated the collar of his shirt in a slick, warm substance.

"Foolish children," Gwydion roared, turning on the pair of them. Silks floated around them, and glittering magic flittered through the air. "Look what you've done!"

But Blaze didn't flinch. Fable's vision blurred, but he saw the dragon shift back to the boy, and rush over to him with brows knitted in concern. Hands flitted over him as if to check for wounds. "Mage, are you all right?"

Fable opened his mouth to speak, but nothing came out, just a croak. Something was wrong. Something was broken. Something was—he couldn't seem to think of the right word. Bright colored scarves and the soft jingle of jewelry followed him as he floated in and out of consciousness. The next moment he was laid out on the soft grass.

"Do something," Blaze demanded. There was something strained and raw about the dragon's voice now with all of his rage evaporated like so much mist. "Fix him."

"I can't," Gwydion stated.

"What do you mean you can't? You're a witch! Witches fix people!" Blaze's frustrated words echoed and rang in Fable's ears. He wondered why the dragon even cared. He didn't even know Fable's name.

"Not when they have bleeding on the brain. Maybe you should have thought of that before you threw him like a rag-doll," Gwydion shot back; eyes narrowed dangerously.

"I didn't mean to," Blaze's voice warbled, and his shoulders sagged. "I lost my temper."

"Yes, you seem to do quite a lot of that, don't you child?" Gwydion mocked. "I can't fix him, but he asked me for something before you arrived. I can give him that."

"Give him what?"

Gwydion's lips twisted in wry amusement. "The ability to tame a dragon." The wind rose and glittered with golden magic, ruffling Fable's matted curls, and cooling the slick of blood on the back of his neck. Leaning forward, Gwydion whispered into his ear so lowly that Fable was sure Blaze didn't hear. "I give you the power to tame the dragon. But know this, you will live every day with that purpose, and your soul shall know no true rest until it is done. Good luck, my boy." Then they pressed their full lips gently to Fable's forehead. "There, that ought to do it."

"Tame a dragon? What does that even mean?"

Fable felt consciousness slipping away as he grew colder. He thought vaguely, *this must be what dying feels like. I hope Grandfather is all right.*

Gwydion's voice sounded more and more muffled, but Fable forced himself to listen. "And for burning down my home," Gwydion rounded on the dragon, poking one long fingernail into Blaze's chest. "You will not be able to control your dragon powers at all until you can learn to control your temper." Angry, flitting, red magic flowed from the pointed finger into Blaze's chest. "Till then, anything you touch in anger will turn to ash."

The last thing Fable heard before he finally lost his grip on reality—or life, perhaps—was Blaze sputtering obscenities at Gwydion.

TWO

They held a funeral for the mage a week later. Blaze learned that his name had been Fable, and he'd been a bright-eyed, young man who made everyone around him happy. It was a foolish, sentimental affair meant to honor the dead, but all it seemed to Blaze to be was a way for those who hadn't cared for the boy in life to save face. Many cried, including the idiot warrior who had shoved the mage that first time Blaze had spoken to him. Blaze watched from the trees as Fable's lifeless body was pushed out to sea on a raft before being set aflame. A feeling of disgust twisted in his gut.

"Stupid humans," he murmured under his breath, ducking back into the shadows.

He vowed not to go back to the caves after that. He'd move on, find another part of the world to hide away in. After all, the one person who may have been his friend was gone now, and he had little hope that those in the village would be kind to him after what happened. Maybe he'd get far enough away from the human race that he could be left alone—in peace—finally.

HE DIDN'T FIND PEACE. For humans—unlike his own species that was quickly dwindling—spread across the world in all shapes, sizes, and colors. And it wasn't but a year before a group of foolish young men stumbled upon him in his most recent hiding place.

Only three, Blaze thought as he spread his giant wings, ready to fend them off with ease. "One lick of flame, that's all it ought to take to send them running home to mommy," he muttered to himself. But as Blaze inhaled deeply, readying to send a short burst that would scare them into the hills, an odd coolness stilled his breath. A moment later, on the exhale, all he released was a puff of smoke.

As the smoke floated upwards, the three young men dissolved into raucous laughter. "A dragon who can't breathe fire?" one of them chortled, finding it hard to breathe.

"It's almost not even worth the trouble," another wheezed, holding his stomach.

Blaze snarled, lashing out at them. He may not have his fire, but his claws worked. Striking out at them with talons sharp as razors, he ended their laughter, and soon the trio was on their guard again. A roar filled the air, shaking the cave walls, when one got lucky and sank his blade into Blaze's tail. Blaze lunged for the little human—fully intent on dispatching of it—when a limp, freckled face flashed through his mind, and stilled his movements entirely.

It only took a moment for the memory to flash across his mind, but a moment is all they needed. The leader of the trio took his chance, blade slicing through the air to scrape off a scale on the dragon's unprotected chest.

"I got it!" one of them crowed in victory, holding up the shimmering scale like it was a trophy.

"Let's go," another rushed, and they turned to scamper off with their prize.

A soft whine left the dragon as he slumped back further into his cave to lick his wounds. Once he'd shifted back into the shape of a boy, Blaze found a small patch of skin on his chest scraped clean away, oozing crimson blood onto his pale skin. "Damn humans," he rasped to himself, heating his hand with whatever residual flame remained in his body to cauterize the wound. "Damn humans. Damn witch."

WITHOUT THE ABILITY TO blow flames, Blaze kept to his human form more and more often. That human had been right, what use *was* there in a dragon who couldn't breathe fire? Without it, hunting became more hassle than it was worth, and at some point, he started wandering the villages below in search of food. With no money to speak of, he quickly resorted to stealing to keep himself fed.

It was on one such excursion some years after Fable's funeral—though Blaze had quite lost track of how many— that what Gwydion had said came back into focus.

The smell of fresh bread filled the air, causing Blaze's stomach to growl loudly. Amber eyes flicked this way and that. They caught on a shock of brown curls dipped low over a book, not paying attention as the man walked. Another loud rumble left Blaze's belly, and he snatched up a loaf of bread before walking away calmly in the same direction the young man was heading. He'd learned some time ago that the best way to get away with something was to act like nothing was wrong.

The young man—seeming to notice that Blaze was following him—looked up from his book. Blue and green eyes met Blaze's for a moment, and recognition dawned instantly in Blaze's mind.

"Fable?" Blaze growled, the question coming off more threatening than he'd intended.

Fable *eeped* softly, eyes widening, and then he walked more quickly to lose the man following him.

Blaze sped up to keep pace, not thinking about the action. It had been so long since he'd seen those eyes. What was this? Fable hadn't survived. *This must be some kind of reincarnation,* Blaze's mind supplied. So would Fable remember him? Would he be able to apologize for what happened? Did he even want to at this point? All humans had done was hurt him in the last several years. But not Fable. "Wait, slow down," he tried to reason with the frightened, young man.

Fable picked up his pace and then a second later, he took off in a sprint. Someone behind them shouted, "Thief! Get that boy! Thief!"

Everything after that happened in slow motion. A soldier ducked out of a nearby pub, having heard the shouts. He lifted his pistol and fired. The crack made Blaze's ears ring. A moment later, Fable stumbled forward with a loud cry. Blaze didn't register his steps before he was on his knees beside the bleeding young man, hunger long forgotten. "Fable? Are you all right?"

Mismatched eyes looked up at him for a moment in confusion, and then recognition dawned on Fable and his eyes narrowed. He remembered. "Get off of me!" he snarled, swatting Blaze away. He coughed into his sleeve, and the crisp white fabric came away bloody.

"Damn it, not again," Blaze hissed. "We have to—"

Another crack cut off his words, and left his ears ringing. At closer range the man's aim was better; this bullet had buried itself in Fable's chest. There was no amount of dragon fire that would fix that, Blaze realized and the horror sunk in that he was about to hold Fable as he died again. Fable collapsed, another cough wracking his body. Blaze reached for the books strewn across the street to save them from the blood.

"I got him," the soldier crowed in victory. "I told you I was getting better! All right, let's get him to the jail."

"Leave him alone!" Blaze barked. Rage sizzled just below the skin. He shifted to put himself between the soldier and Fable, unsure why it mattered now. Fable would die—soon, in fact—but Blaze couldn't help the notion to protect him.

"Get out of the way," the soldier snorted, slamming the butt of his weapon into Blaze's shoulder to force him away. Blaze didn't move. He stayed firm, clutching a book to his chest as the fury rolled up inside of him.

Smoke billowed from his hands, the smell of burnt paper assaulting his nose. When he looked down, he found Fable's books reduced to ash. Wild amber eyes swung up to meet the soldier's, and in a panic, Blaze leaped to his feet and took off. He didn't stop running until he was as deep in his cave as he could go. Back pressed to the hard, jutting surface. It was only then that he realized one of the books had survived his cursed hands. He slid to the floor, drinking in the indecipherable symbols on the cover.

"No more stealing," he promised himself.

BY THE TIME he crossed paths with those eyes again, Blaze had learned to read that little volume—it was a book of poetry—and he led a normal human life. Fable was an old woman then, frail and bent, but those eyes were still the same. Blaze couldn't identify the feeling, but he felt something as they bore into him.

"Watch where you're going, boy," the woman hissed, mismatched eyes narrowed on Blaze in her anger.

"Why don't you watch where *you're* going, you old hag!" Blaze snapped back at her, baring his teeth.

"You should learn to respect you elders!" She swatted him harshly with her cane, stinging his calf.

"And you ought to learn to respect your betters!" he snarled at her. She lashed out with her cane again, aiming for his face this time, Blaze lifted his arm to brush it aside. The impact knocked Fable off balance, and she stumbled out into the nearby street. A carriage careened towards them, unable to stop in time. Blaze didn't have even a second to act. When the driver finally pulled the horse to a stop, it was a hair too late.

AFTER THAT, Blaze vowed to put some distance between himself and Fable—an ocean, in fact. The colonies were duller than he would have thought they would be. He was looking for adventure and new territory, and the colonists were looking to go on witch hunts, but there was no sign of Fable. He took some solace in that, hoping maybe he'd outrun Gwydion's curse.

The Revolution came some time later. Years had blurred together, and Blaze itched for a fight, so he was the first to enlist.

War wasn't new to him; humans had been waging war against one another for as long as he had been alive, but Blaze had never taken part in one before. What was new to him was being shot with something other than an arrow. In the years since humans had invented guns—always looking for a new way to kill each other—Blaze had handily avoided them. Thus, when a musket ball pierced his skin, he found the sensation new, and unpleasant.

"I'm fine," he grunted to his commander, intent on hunkering down, and waiting it out until they had at least cleared the surrounding area. Blaze lifted his musket again, aiming for a red coat in the distance, and fired. The kickback of the weapon slammed into his injured shoulder. "Damn it all to hell," he breathed through the fresh blossom of pain.

"To the medical tent. Now," the commander ordered.

"I don't need to go to the bloody medical tent! I hit him, didn't I?" Blaze shouted back in irritation.

"Now," the man hissed; bushy eyebrows narrowed.

In a fit of aggravation, Blaze threw down his weapon and stomped off in the tent's direction, not bothering to look behind him, or cover himself just in case. What would it matter? They couldn't kill a dragon.

The tent was too small for the number of injured men inside. With the cots all full, many had been forced to sit in the dirt while they waited their turn. A nurse looked up at the movement of the tent flap, eyes locking on Blaze's. One blue, one green—Blaze felt panic seep into his bones. "Take a seat, I'll be right with you," the woman said briskly.

How the hell did that bastard find me again? Blaze wondered, standing there with his eyes wide as they followed Fable around the tent for a moment.

"Didn't you hear her, man? Sit down," someone urged,

shoving him into a free spot alongside a cot where a man laid, not moving.

Despite the difference in gender, Fable looked almost the same as she had the first time Blaze had met her. Her eyes were a little wider, cheeks a little rounder, but the color was the same, and she was still covered in freckles. How long had it been? Blaze tried to count the years but quickly lost them when pain shot through his shoulder.

"What the hell was that for?" He bared his teeth at the woman suddenly beside him, poking around his wound with deft fingers.

"We must get the bullet out," Fable said reasonably, looking down her thin nose at him.

"How about we don't and say we didn't?" He held his hand over the still bleeding injury to keep her from poking at it further.

"We remove the bullet, or we risk it migrating towards your heart," Fable's words were calm but stern. "Now, are you going to be a baby about this, or are you going to let me do my job?"

"A baby?" Blaze sputtered. "Do you talk to all of your patients that way?"

"Only the ones who act like infants," Fable answered with a little shrug. Her hands made quick work of unbuttoning his uniform so she could better see the damage on his shoulder. "Gauze," she ordered, and someone handed it to her.

"Best to let her get it over with," someone from his right muttered under their breath. "Then you can rest."

"I don't need rest." Blaze turned to glare at the redheaded stranger beside him.

"Me either." He smirked at Blaze as if they were both in

on some joke. Amber eyes flicked to take in the slightly pointed ears carefully tucked beneath his long hair.

Fae, Blaze thought irritably. *Wonderful.* But he didn't have more than the passing thought to spare as Fable had begun digging for the bullet, eliciting a loud curse from the dragon.

When all was said and done, Blaze leaned back against a wooden trunk, panting roughly and holding his bandaged shoulder. Fable had finished her work and skipped off to help her other patients.

"She must hate you," the redheaded fae whispered as if he were confiding some great secret to Blaze. "Usually, she gives the men whiskey before digging out bullets."

"Well, aren't I lucky." Blaze's eyes followed Fable around the tent, unable to look anywhere else.

"Eero." The redhead extended his hand in introduction.

Blaze looked down at it, and then back up at Eero, his lip curling in disgust before he growled low, and threatening in the back of his throat. "I don't talk to fae trash."

"Of course not," Eero offered cheerfully. "You also don't get involved with human wars that have absolutely nothing to do with you either. Right?"

Blaze refused to dignify that with an answer in favor of returning his focus to Fable. She seemed in her element, flitting from bed to bed, to help with whatever she could. Blaze wondered if that was what Fable had been like in his first life—if he'd always been so damned kind. An image of a freckled boy delivering some kind of salve to a house-bound, old woman flashed in Blaze's mind. Yes, Fable had always been so kind. Which is exactly what had gotten him killed in the first place. Idiot.

A week later, his troop moved on, and Fable stayed

behind to clean up. Blaze didn't see her again during the war, but Eero stuck to him like glue from then on.

BLAZE CAUGHT glimpses of Fable a few more times in the years that came, but always carefully avoided him.

THE TITANIC WOULD BE a marvel of modern engineering, and Blaze had to see it. Humans were always outdoing themselves. Over the years, they had impressed him over and over with their ingenuity. Even without magic, they had accomplished so much.

"Soon they'll all be flying around, just like you," Eero teased as they lounged in two chairs on the open expanse of sunlit deck. Over the years—despite Blaze's best efforts—he'd been unable to shake the fae. Eero insisted that they were friends—Blaze wasn't even sure what that meant.

"They've already built something that can do that." Blaze rolled his eyes, not bothering to lower his newspaper to shoot Eero an irritated look. He had always kept up on the latest advances in human technology, and when the Wright brothers announced their fantastic flying machine, he'd been more than a little impressed. "Now, go bother someone else, I'm reading."

Eero quirked a brow at him. "This whole ship to explore, and you're reading?" Eero's tone was incredulous, and perhaps a little annoyed.

Blaze couldn't be bothered. "That's what I said."

With a snort, Eero stood from his chair, snatched the

newspaper from Blaze, and took off at an all-out run across the open deck.

"You bastard! Get back here!" Blaze roared, leaping to his feet to chase the redhead. He dashed after the other man, but fae being lighter on their feet, Eero stayed one step ahead. Eero ducked around a corner, and Blaze followed. "Eero! Give me back my damn paper you piece of—" His words were cut off when Blaze collided with someone else. Stumbling back a little, he somehow maintained his footing.

"Why don't you watch where you're going?" the person scolded from where they sat on the deck, their curly brown head ducked to glare at the worn knees of their trousers. Then their eyes caught sight of Blaze's polished shoes, and followed them up, up, up till mismatched eyes met Blaze's fiery amber ones. "Oh," the young man gasped, his cheeks flushing brightly.

Strawberry blond brows pinched together, Blaze's mouth twisting into a sneer. "Maybe you should watch where *you're* going, you filthy little mongrel," Blaze hissed threateningly. He stormed off, vowing to make Eero pay for this, leaving Fable sitting on the deck looking dumbfounded after him.

Eero found him some hours later, hiding in their private rooms, scowling at a pile of ash on the table. "What did you disintegrate now?" Eero asked, flopping down across from him. Blaze noted that Eero no longer had his newspaper, and his scowl deepened.

"A pillow," Blaze grumbled in response. His fist clenched and unclenched on the table. "I just don't know how that little shit keeps finding me. I've moved countries. I've changed my name. I never stay in one place for over ten years, tops. I'm in the middle of the bloody ocean, for God's sake!"

"What little—Oooooh. This is about the mage." Eero nodded in understanding. "Well, it's probably about that curse, isn't it? He can't exactly 'tame a dragon' if he's not around it."

Blaze slammed his hand on the table, and the lacquered surface sizzled.

"Oi! Don't light the table on fire! I'm not paying for that!"

Blaze tore his hand away quickly. Too late, he'd left a charred and smoking handprint behind. "Damn it."

"You're paying for that," Eero sighed.

THE NEXT TIME Blaze caught sight of those eyes, it was as he ran to a lifeboat. In the chaos, they shoved him and Eero onto a boat, and Blaze lost sight of the mop of brown hair. Later, Blaze searched the list of the dead for Fable's name but didn't find it.

BLAZE SAW those eyes many more times over the years once he gave up trying to outrun the curse. Instead, he put his focus on finding outlets for his aggression—never able to tamp down the rage, but at least able to channel it. He worked for the mob in the 20s, where Fable's eyes appeared in the face of a flapper at a speakeasy. Then he took up boxing, and Fable's eyes were there in a child in the crowd. Each time ended in disaster.

After a while, he and Eero settled in as firefighters in New York. "Sometimes, you gotta fight fire with fire," Eero had said one day during training, and Blaze figured that was right. He never felt so focused and in control as when he was on the job. At least as a firefighter, he was helping people.

THE ALARM RANG LOUDLY, jolting Blaze out of a string of memories it was likely best he didn't entertain. Suiting up and leaping onto the truck was second nature to him now, and they were barreling through the crowded city streets in no time. When they reached the building, relief washed over Blaze. It was an old factory that looked to be closed for remodeling—probably going to become a market or some such as these things do. The chained fence around it should have kept out any homeless people, which meant they just needed to get the fire under control.

With a nod, several men headed inside to clear the floors. Blaze—with Eero hot on his heels—took the upper levels. They checked room after room, and were just about to head back down, when a soft whimper reached Blaze's ears. He stilled. "Did you hear that?"

Eero stopped, listening to the sounds of the surrounding building. "I don't hear anything. What is it?"

"I think it's whimpering." Spinning clumsily on his heel, Blaze headed back. The heavy equipment made him clunky, and really, he didn't need it to protect himself from a fire but trying telling humans that. Soft whimpers led him to a closet at the end of the hall. He flung the door open to find a small, scruffy looking dog cowering at the back of it. "It's all right, buddy," Blaze soothed, crouching low to reach for the animal. "I'm gonna get you out of here." The dog did its best to wriggle away, its back pressing to the wall as it shook in terror. Blaze took a calming breath, and kept reaching, ignoring the all too familiar expression of being trapped on the creature's face.

"Hurry!" Eero shouted down the hall. "I don't know how much longer these floors will hold up!"

"Just about there," Blaze grunted, grabbing the creature by its scruff. "Gotcha." He scooped it up and settled it against his chest, and jogged back to the steps. Outside, the hot summer air felt cool against his skin compared to the flames inside. He pulled the dog away from himself to get a better look at it. It looked all right, no burns or cuts, but it was panting hard, either from fear, or struggling to breathe. "We need to get it to a vet," Eero said.

Blaze nodded, already reaching for the phone tucked in his pocket as they loaded into the truck. "Where do you take your lizard?"

"Chameleon," Eero corrected, but he pulled out his phone and sent the details to Blaze.

"Whatever."

BLAZE LEFT AS SOON as they reached the station. The vet wasn't far, but he didn't want to take any chances as the little dog was breathing heavier. "Hang on buddy, we're almost there," he hushed soothingly, petting the scruffy fur.

The waiting room was jam-packed when he walked in, but Blaze only took a cursory look around before heading to the counter. "Do you have an appointment?" the young girl at the desk asked, not looking up from her computer screen.

"No, bu—"

"We don't take walk-ins," she cut him off without letting him finish.

"I understand that, but I need to speak to—"

"Don't matter. We don't take walk-ins," she cut him off again.

Blaze took a deep, calming breath, before narrowing his eyes on her. "It's an emergency."

"Then you gotta go to the emergency clinic up in Midtown."

A muscle in Blaze's jaw ticked dangerously. "I'm not bloody going to Midtown!" he shouted, startling the little dog in his arms. A head peeked out from a room up the hall, but Blaze took no notice. "I just saved this damn mutt from a fire; he needs emergency medical attention! NOW!" Blaze's volume had escalated into a roar very much reminiscent of the dragon he was. The little dog shivered in fear.

"I've got it Karen," a calm voice announced as footsteps padded quickly down the hall.

"You're supposed to be on break, Doctor Alperen," Karen insisted. "If Doctor Guthrie finds out you skipped lu—"

"This is an emergency," he cut her off. "Follow me." The man tilted his head toward the narrow hall lined in doors. Blaze stomped after him towards an empty exam room, only half paying attention to the vet as he tried to shush and quiet the panicking dog in his arms. "Set him on the table."

Blaze held the dog for a moment longer before settling it gently down onto the metal table. It whimpered softly when he pulled his hands away, so he kept one on its paw to provide as much comfort as he could. He knew that sound—had heard it more times from himself than he'd care to admit, and it broke his heart to hear it from another living creature. "I'm still here," he whispered soothingly.

After grabbing some supplies, Doctor Alperen turned around and finally met Blaze's eyes.

One blue, one green.

Shit.

He. They. Them. Doctor Alperen—or whatever the humans had named them this time—never remembered the dragon, but the dragon always remembered him. The mage had no recollection of the centuries-old feud, or all the times they had met in the past. Blaze could recall every chance meeting, every argument, every eventual death. And here they were—again. Bile rose in his throat, but he forced it down.

Damn it.

THREE

Fable was silent in his work—examining the dog, administering fluids, and oxygen. When the dog had calmed and seemed to be breathing better, he leaned back on his heels to smile at the man who'd brought it in. Mismatched eyes flickered over him to drink him in. A firefighter, if the logo on his shirt, and what he'd said was a sign. A handsome one at that. But that was neither here nor there, Fable reminded himself.

"We can keep him here until his family gets out of the hospital," Fable offered with what he hoped was a comforting smile.

The fireman seemed to jerk out of a trance and frowned as he shook his head. "He doesn't have a family," he rumbled, voice low and gravelly.

Fable blinked. "What?"

"He's a stray. He was in an abandoned building." The man explained, his strawberry blond brows creasing in thought. Then he closed his eyes, took a deep breath, and reopened them as if he'd decided something. "I'm keeping him."

"You don't have to do that, we're more than capable of finding someone who will take good care of him. He can stay here and receive treatment until he's on his feet, and then we'll send him to one of our foster homes until we can adopt him out," Fable reasoned softly. "He's not your responsibility." It was an admirable thing to want to keep an injured animal that he'd just saved, but pets were a big responsibility. Especially pets who would require medical attention. "He'll be a lot of work."

"So?" The blond snorted, amber eyes flaring up in a challenge.

"So, you don't just take that on lightly. Trust me, we'll find him a good home. *I'll* find him a good home," Fable tried to assure him.

"Do you think I can't do it?" the man growled, baring his teeth in a way much like a cornered, injured, and frightened animal might. Anger flashed across his face, contorting what was once handsome into something dangerous and frightening. "Do I look incapable to you?"

"No!" Fable squeaked, raising his hands to calm the other down. He didn't want a fight, and he could hear the little dog growing restless at the angry energy between them. "I just—I just—This is a lot of work, is all."

"And I said that was fine! What do I have to do, hire a damn skywriter? I'm adopting the damn mutt!" his voice echoed off the cement walls, and made Fable jerk.

Swallowing roughly, Fable nodded. "All—all right then. I'll just get a chart started for him." He spun on his heel, putting some distance between himself and the furious firefighter as he dug out a new folder and pen. "I'll need your name," he mumbled, eyes fixed on the paper before him instead of the glare that could cut diamonds being leveled at him.

"Blaze," the man grunted.

"Last name, please?" Fable scribbled it down, focusing on breathing calmly. It would do him no good to get worked up over this, or to let his own temper get the better of him.

"Ender."

"All right, Mr. Ender, I'll just need you to fill out a form at the front desk with your address and contact information. I will also send you home with some instructions for your new dog's care along with antibiotics. He seems to be suffering from flash blindness, but that should go away in a few days. Till then, maybe get some puppy pads?" Fable began jotting everything down on a clean sheet of paper.

"Puppy pads?" Blaze asked, his nose curling up as his anger melted away into something else entirely.

"Yeah, they sell them at the pet store. They're in case he has an accident in the house."

"Write it down," Blaze instructed, tapping the paper a little harder than necessary. "And some food recommendations and shit." He sounded unsure. Fable looked up from the paper to examine the man before him for a moment. With the anger stripped away, uncertainty and earnestness had settled in. This was a man who wanted to help but wasn't sure how.

Fable blinked at Blaze, frowning a little as he shook himself mentally. "You have owned a dog before, haven't you?"

Amber eyes flicked down to the table where the scruffy dog had curled up against Blaze's stomach to sleep. "No, I haven't," he admitted, his tone barely above a whisper. The sound felt weirdly familiar, though Fable knew they'd never met before.

More blinking followed, as he tried to shake the weird sense of déjà vu. Fable exhaled, forcing his shoulders to relax, and turned to grab a pamphlet from the rack behind him. "This should help. And I uh..." He frowned to himself, this was a stupid idea, and he wasn't exactly sure why he was doing it. He chalked it up to feeling bad for the poor, white and brown speckled mutt, and scribbled his number on a blank space on the back. "This is my personal number. You can call me if you have questions. Or text. Just don't hire a skywriter," he teased gently despite himself and slid the pamphlet over along with his scrawled instructions. "I'll be happy to help any way that I can."

The firefighter looked up from the little dog to blink at Fable for a moment, brows creased in confusion. "Do you often give your patients your personal number?" he asked in a slow, measured tone.

"Do you often keep the animals you save in fires?" Fable fired back in a sassy tone. Was he flirting? Why was he flirting? Not two seconds ago he'd written this guy off as a complete asshole!

Full lips turned up at the corners, and Blaze scoffed, seeming suddenly amused. Fable had to admit, that was a better look for him. "Right then. See you, doc."

Fable nodded. "See the girl at the front desk to fill the prescription and settle up about your bill. It was nice meeting you, Mr. Ender."

Blaze scooped up the little dog, turned on his heel, and strode out, leaving Fable to slump back against the table. His hands scrubbed at the back of his neck, still not sure what just happened, and why he'd acted that way.

"Oh, hello, handsome firefighter, here's my number," a voice giggled from the door to his right. Fable yanked it open to glare down at the other vet, who stumbled forward as if she'd had her ear pressed to the door to eavesdrop.

She probably had. "Aura, how long were you snooping?"

"Long enough." She shrugged, sliding into the room. "He must have been hella handsome to score your personal line for 'questions'." Aura lifted her fingers to put air quotes around the word questions with a knowing smirk. Then she peeked out of the room to look down the hall, presumably at where Mr. Ender was settling his bill. "Oh, look at that butt," she whistled.

"Aura," Fable hissed, grabbing her by the wrist to yank her back into the room. "That is entirely inappropriate."

"So is flirting with your patients. But you don't see me scolding you." She brushed him off with ease. Then, bouncing on her toes so that her bob waved slightly, cheeks reddened with excitement, she asked, "If you don't want him, can I have him?"

"Don't you have puppies to deliver, or something? Go bother someone else." Fable gave her a little shove back to the door she'd just come through so he could head to his office. He needed a minute to breathe, to regain himself, to distance himself from Blaze Ender, and above all, to ponder if he wanted the firefighter to use that number or not. "I need to finish my lunch."

"Uh, huh. Sure." Aura nodded but disappeared through the door to leave him to his thoughts.

FABLE HAD JUST DOZED—NESTLED in between a purring cat and two snoring dogs—when the loud ringer of his phone jerked him awake. Mismatched eyes narrowed on the device through the dark, before he flopped a hand onto it to pull it to him. "I don't recognize this number," he sighed, scrubbing at his eyes. The cat beside him hissed at the brightly lit screen. "Yeah, me too, Jiji," he grumbled, sitting up a little to at least sound awake, before hitting the green button, and lifting it to his ear. With a deep inhale, he readied himself to shout at the telemarketer that must inevitably be on the other end.

"What do I do if he won't eat?" the rushed, almost panicked, question stilled any anger in his throat. "Doctor Alperen?" the voice asked.

"Who is this? I'm not on call tonight," Fable grunted, sitting up more in bed. "Doctor Guthrie is taking calls tonight. Did Karen get us mixed up on the switchboard again?" Fable groused, scrubbing his curly hair into a mess he may never get a comb through again. "I swear, that girl, she's suppo—"

"It's Blaze Ender. The firefighter from earlier," the voice responded, sounding a little irritated with Fable's muttering. "You told me to call you if I had any problems."

"Huh?" Fable asked before his mind caught up to what the voice was saying. Then he remembered the little Jack Russell mix with the flash blindness, and the strawberry blond firefighter with cold amber eyes, and a scar down the side of his face. "Mr. Ender, right," he said more to himself than to the voice on the other end.

"Yeah, that guy," Blaze snorted derisively.

Fable bristled at the tone, but turned his attention quickly back to the situation at hand. He took a moment to sort through the information he had on the little dog in his mind. Muttering under his breath as he remembered the dog's weight, diagnosis, fluids had been administered—

"Oi!" Blaze shouted from the other end of the phone. "I asked a damn question."

"No need to be rude, Mr. Ender," Fable scolded softly.

"Right, whatever. Why won't the little shit eat?" Blaze sounded frustrated—perhaps a little worried—but mostly frustrated.

Fable pinched the bridge of his nose and sighed. He didn't particularly want to deal with an angry patient in the middle of the night. It seemed he had little choice in the matter now. Why had he given Blaze his personal number again? Oh right, the earnestness. Damn it. "What did you feed him?"

"The shit you told me to feed him," Blaze grunted. "I'm not an idiot. I know how to follow instructions."

"Has he had any water?" Fable didn't know what possessed him, but he was already climbing from the warmth of his bed, earning a glare from a disgruntled Jiji who had been curled up on his legs.

"Doesn't look like it."

"Any vomiting?" he asked, tugging a well-worn sweater on over his thin t-shirt, and slipping into a pair of hard-soled slippers.

"No. He just doesn't seem interested in the food," Blaze was still speaking directly into the phone, but something about his voice sounded distant now. Like he was scared.

Fable checked the time—midnight—he frowned. "This time of night, the train schedule will be all wonky," he devolved into his usual muttering. "And the cabs will be around the bars, just have to call for a car I guess."

"What?" Blaze asked, suddenly not distant at all, and much more annoyed. It was probably the muttering, Fable had been told many times it was irritating, but it was a hard habit to break. "What the hell are you talking about?"

Fable wasn't listening, though. Instead, he had focused his attention on loading a couple cans of wet dog food into his messenger bag along with a syringe kit, just in case. He muttered to himself, ticking items off his mental list as he loaded them into the bag.

"Hey!" The shout jerked Fable out of his thoughts, and he frowned deeply. Right, he'd been talking to someone.

"Oh, uh, right. Text me your address," Fable instructed, only half paying attention as he ran down the list again.

"My what?" Blaze growled into the phone.

Fable huffed, scrubbing at his eyes. "Your address, Mr. Ender."

"What for?"

"I'm coming over to give your dog a once over, and try to get him to eat something. Now, are you going to cooperate, or am I going to call the office and get your address off your files?" Fable seethed, arguing over this was a waste of time. The longer they screwed around doing that, the less sleep he'd get.

"I feel that's probably a gross misuse of your position as a veterinarian," Blaze countered snarkily.

"I have to be into the office at 6am tomorrow morning to prep for a surgery. This is not a discussion. Send me your address so I can get back home to my bed." Fable clenched his jaw, irritation making his freckled cheeks hot. Who the hell did this guy think he was, anyway? He called in the middle of the night, and had the gall to be affronted, when all Fable was doing was trying to help his dog!

"Fine," Blaze snorted. The line went quiet for a moment, and then Fable felt his phone buzz against his ear. "Sent. See you soon, doc," he huffed before hanging up.

"Asshole," Fable grumbled to himself.

HE WAS STILL GRUMBLING BITTERLY when the car pulled up outside of an older apartment building in the Lower East Side. "Is this some kind of hookup? Should I wait?" the driver—a woman in her twenties who had been nothing but polite—asked.

Fable resisted the urge to balk at the mere idea of a hookup with Mr. Ender of all people, but shook his head. "That's sweet of you, but no. I'm okay."

She flicked her eyes over his pajama-clad form for a moment. "Right."

With that, he shut the door and headed to the apartment building. It was easy to find Mr. Ender's name on the list and hit the buzzer. Blaze didn't call down to check who it was, before buzzed Fable into the building.

"I could have been a serial killer or something," Fable muttered to himself as he headed down the hall towards the apartment number Blaze had sent.

Several muffled curse words followed his knock, and soon the door was flung open to reveal a very muscular, very scarred, very shirtless chest. Fable blinked at the sun-kissed skin for a moment, then forced his eyes up to meet the narrowed, amber eyes a head above him. "Come in," Blaze grunted, stepping out of the way.

Inside the small apartment was a beat-up futon, a large tv, and scattered all over the floor was more dog toys than Fable had ever seen in his life. It would have been endearing, if Fable weren't so utterly shocked. "Did you like—just —buy one of everything the pet store had?" he asked, eyes bouncing from squeaky toys, to balls, to stuffed animals.

Blaze shrugged, kicking a bright red dragon stuffed toy out of his way with a socked foot. "I didn't know what he'd like."

"That's—" Fable stopped, searching for the right word

to use. "Oddly sweet," he finished with a little laugh and wide-eyed wonder. Could the man be any more of a contradiction?

"Whatever. You said you could get the dipshit to eat?"

Fable nodded, pulling his messenger back around to where he could better dig through it to retrieve a can of wet dog food. "Where is he?"

Blaze sighed. He took a couple quick steps over to the futon, dodging toys in his wake, and flopped down on his belly to stare beneath it. "He's been hiding under here since we got home," his voice sounded tired, and worried, as he pointed to a ball of fluff next to some balls Blaze must have thought would draw him out.

Fable dropped his bag on the futon, and flopped down beside him, to peer at the dog. "Hey there, little buddy. Remember me?"

"His name is Bakugo," Blaze informed him with a grunt.

Fable turned his head to look at Blaze in surprise. "Like from the anime?" he asked, an unbidden smile crinkling at his eyes. *The hits just keep coming, don't they?*

"No, like the Elizabethan playwright," Blaze scoffed, rolling his eyes. "Of course, like the anime. Can you get him to fracking come out and eat, or what? I'm not paying you to sit around and criticize my taste in media."

Fable shook his head, swallowing a laugh as he pushed himself to his feet. "Where's your microwave?"

"Kitchen's through there." Blaze gestured vaguely over his shoulder as he scooted himself deeper under the couch, muttering something Fable couldn't make out through the couch.

Fable took his time picking across the room to avoid stepping on any of the toys. Through the door, he found a small kitchen. It took him a minute of digging through the hand full of cabinets to find a plate, smack the food onto it, and throw it in the microwave for a few seconds. When he returned to Blaze, the broad-shouldered man had somehow gotten himself chest-deep under the futon. *Aura was right. He does have a rather nice bottom,* Fable thought idly. Then he shook that thought aside.

"Get out from under there, you're going to get yourself bit," Fable scowled.

"I've almost got him," Blaze's voice called back, muffled by the furniture.

"Yeah, well, you'll scare him more than he already is. I'm not treating a dog bite tonight." Fable nudged the man's hip with his foot. "If you move your ass, he'll come out on his own."

Blaze slid back out, and sat up to narrow his amber eyes at Fable. "What the hell is that? It smells disgusting."

Fable huffed, rolling his eyes. "Trust me." He set the plate on the floor, just outside of where Bakugo was hiding, grabbed a magazine off the coffee table, and fanned the smell towards the little dog.

"He's not coming out for that—it smells like ass," Blaze snorted in disgust.

"Shut up, and watch," Fable hissed. Mismatched eyes trained on the space under the futon. The sound of little claws scraping the hardwood floor preceded a snout emerging from the depths. "There he is," Fable whispered, relieved. He saw movement out of the corner of his eye, and held up a hand to stop Blaze. "Not yet, let him get comfortable with his surroundings for a minute. We'll deal with getting some water into him soon."

Blaze sat back on his heels; eyes wide as he watched the dog scarf down the food. "How did you know that would work?"

"I'm a vet," Fable answered as if it were obvious. "The fire must have distorted his sense of smell. It should go back to normal with his vision in a few days. Till then, I have a couple more cans of that in my bag."

WHEN BAKUGO HAD LICKED the plate clean, Fable stuck a bowl of water under his nose, carefully splashing some up onto his muzzle. This encouraged the dog to drink a little.

"All right," Fable said as he threw the messenger bag back over his shoulder, and called another car. "He should be fine for fluids now, and just keep trying with the kibble. If he doesn't seem to go for it after an hour, heat a can of the soft food."

Blaze nodded thoughtfully, his hand petting the dog gently in his arms. "Thanks for coming by," the words came from gritted teeth, as if he'd never really said 'thank you' in his life—Fable would believe it.

Fable shrugged. "It's my job. Besides, I can't ever say 'no' to a face like this, can I Bakugo?" Fable cooed at the dog, scratching behind his ears, and receiving a short rumble of appreciation for his trouble. "I'll set up a follow-up visit for him when I get into the office tomorrow, so we can check that he's in the all-clear, and get his shots out of the way."

"Will they just—" Blaze faded off, his brow wrinkled as if he wasn't sure what he'd been about to ask.

"They'll call you to let you know in the afternoon," Fable supplied for him.

"Okay." Blaze turned to shut the door, then stopped a moment later. "It'll be with you?"

Fable quirked a brow. He hadn't considered whether Blaze would want to continue with him being Bakugo's vet or not. Most people didn't seem to realize they had a choice in the matter. "Unless you want a different vet. If you decide you do, let them know when they call. I won't be offended."

"Right," Blaze muttered. "I can umm... call you if he has any more problems, right?"

"Yeah," Fable offered him a wide smile. "Good night, Mr. Ender." He chuckled softly to himself, turning on his heel to head back down to the waiting car.

THAT NIGHT, after Fable had settled into his bed, his dreams were a wash of strange flashes. A tiny room on a ship, the cold, dark ocean engulfing him. He woke the next morning shivering, and aching from the phantom pains of his body seizing up from hypothermia.

FOUR

The events of the previous evening played through Blaze's mind over and over on repeat for much of the following day, and didn't stop even as he slouched into the couch of the station break room. A full conversation with Fable left a feeling of strangeness in Blaze's gut. It wasn't wrong per se, just unusual. He realized, belatedly, that he'd never had a conversation with the mage before. At least not one that hadn't ended in Fable's untimely death. He still wasn't sure how to feel about it, and if he should worry for Fable's safety now, or not.

One thing he had determined was whose fault this whole mess was. Eero. Eero, and his moronic big mouth, and vet recommendation. If it weren't for Eero, perhaps he'd have been able to avoid Fable in this lifetime.

"Wait, so you kept the dog?" Eero asked, as he came into the break room, pulling Blaze from his thoughts to face the target of his newly acquired ire. The redhead narrowed his eyes on the little mutt sprawled out against Blaze's thigh, snoring loudly.

Blaze's eyes flicked up; the rage that had simmered all

day lit into an inferno at the sight of Eero's neatly coifed man-bun. The magazine in his hands—something about cars—crumpled into ashes, causing Eero to wince. "Why didn't you tell me?" Blaze's question rumbled low and threatening.

"Tell you what?" Eero's brown eyes had gone wide with confusion, but no trace of fear lingered within them. *Maybe he didn't know*, Blaze tried to rationalize, but the dragon within snapped, and snarled. *He had to have known!*

"Why didn't you tell me that Fable worked at that vet office!" Blaze shouted more than asked. Despite the noise, none of the other men seemed to take notice of Blaze's anger. It had become commonplace around the station, and so long as he didn't destroy anything important—again—the other men left him to it.

"What?" Eero asked, his almond-shaped eyes blinking in confusion. "Wait, Fable? You mean the—" he trailed off, waving his fingers in the air in an odd way that Blaze could only assume Eero thought implied magic.

"Yes, that Fable," Blaze ground out. He clenched his jaw to keep from shouting again.

"Dude," Eero exhaled, dropping onto the couch beside Bakugo which drew an irritated growl from the little dog. "That's weird. He totally didn't work there before."

Blaze snorted, and grabbed another magazine at random from the pile on the table. He opened it to glare holes into its pages—ignoring the over-bright picture of what seemed to be a blanket made entirely from yarn—but said nothing else.

Eero's red brows creased as he considered this news, then he snapped his fingers in triumph. "Oh, that's right! Aura said they were getting a new vet in. Someone she went to school with was moving into the city from further upstate. Must have been him."

"Fan-fracking-tastic."

"Maybe you could ask Gwydion to like—I dunno—make him go away, or something?" Eero suggested hopefully. They had had this talk before, the second time Blaze had run into Fable. Eero knew what it meant. He also knew that the whole curse pissed Blaze off more than anything ever had. It was because of that idiotic, self-righteous, freckled mage that Blaze could no longer control his flames.

"They won't do that," Blaze spat, flipping through the magazine to skim pages of scarves and hats. "Gwydion never does anything they don't want to, and this is their curse, so they won't undo it now."

"Then why don't you just ask for another vet?"

Blaze didn't bother to answer that, mostly because he didn't have an answer. Would it matter if he found a different vet? Wouldn't Fable just find him another way? As Eero had once pointed out, Fable couldn't tame a dragon that wasn't around, so they were constantly drawn together.

"It's funny, you know," Eero said with a grin.

"No, it's not."

"Yeah, it kind of is," Eero insisted. "It's like Gwydion stuck you both in a giant 'get along' shirt, and won't let you out until you learn to behave."

"A what?" Blaze looked up from the glossy pages full of words like 'half-double crochet' and 'treble crochet', to glare at Eero. "What in God's name is a 'get along' shirt?"

"You know, where a parent puts a big shirt over two kids, and they have to share the same head hole, and each gets an arm? And they can't get out until they learn to get along?"

"I swear, humans get weirder every day." Blaze ducked

his head back to his magazine, refusing to talk about this shit anymore.

BY SOME MIRACLE, Blaze kept Bakugo eating, and drinking until his follow-up visit with Doctor Alperen. The little dog had perked up considerably over the following days and stopped hiding beneath the futon. He'd even taken an interest in some of the toys Blaze had purchased, which was another welcome relief. Bakugo was still using puppy pads, but Blaze knew soon they'd have to work on house training. Blaze even got Bakugo into his carrier for his appointment—not that the struggling, grumbling mutt had been happy about it.

He walked into the full waiting room with a little dog carrier slung over his shoulder. A different girl sat behind the front desk, she had obnoxiously, neon purple hair, and a too-bright smile on her face. "What can I help you with today?" she asked in a too-chipper tone that made Blaze wince.

"Uh, I have an appointment." The little dog whined in terror when a cat in another cage hissed at him. Blaze pulled the strap from his shoulder to hold the bag protectively against his chest until Bakugo quieted. "With Doctor Alperen."

"Name?" Purple-hair asked.

"Mine or his?"

She grinned brightly again—this time all teeth—showing off a mouth full of braces. "Both, actually."

"Blaze Ender, the dog is Bakugo."

Purple-hair typed something into the computer, humming to herself for a moment, then with a nod she turned that metal smile back on Blaze. "Doctor A will be with you shortly. Just take a seat."

Blaze turned back to the full waiting room, his brow furrowing—every seat was taken. So, he took up an empty spot against the wall to wait instead. To pass the time, he pulled out his phone to check for any notifications. No word from the station, but there was a text from Eero.

Eero 2:31 PM
Good luck on your date!!!!!!

Blaze blinked at the text, frowning. He was about to text back and ask Eero what the bloody hell he was talking about, when shouts drew his attention from his phone.

"What do you mean you had to shave her backside?" someone was screaming, as they stomped down the hallway towards the front desk. "You can't just do things like that without clearing it through me first!"

Fable's curly brunette head followed, with his shoulders hiked up to his ears. He removed his glasses to rub at the bridge of his nose tiredly. "I told you exactly what the surgery entailed, Mister Johnson—when we discussed it last week. You even signed a paper that said you understood."

"You did not say it would involve shaving her! She looks hideous! Look at her!" The man held a small fluffy dog's butt up to Fable's face to illustrate his point. "She's so embarrassed! Aren't you embarrassed, pretty girl? You poor thing. The shame!" Blaze wagered the dog was more embarrassed at having its ass stuck in someone's face than being shaved.

"I told you we had to shave the area," Fable argued softly, his jaw clenching in frustration. Blaze smirked a little, wondering how long it would take for the little mage to lose it, and shout back. He'd never really seen Fable turn his ire on anyone but himself, and to be honest, he was eager to glimpse it. "Again, it was all in the paperwork you signed."

"She'll be the laughingstock of her playgroup! Humiliated!" The man ignored Fable's reasonable tone, becoming irater as he advanced on the tall vet threateningly. "You'll pay for this," Mr. Johnson growled, giving Fable a hard shove. The vet stumbled back, and his arm smacked loudly on the corner of the countertop.

That was it. Blaze strode over, setting Bakugo's carrier on the counter near Purple-hair, and out of harm's way before putting himself between Fable and Mr. Johnson. "That's enough, asshole," he growled.

"What are you? His attack dog? I'll say when enough is enough." Mr. Johnson snarled back, craning his neck to glare at the taller man. Blaze's hands curled into fists. He could feel the fire welling up just under the surface, heating his palms to near burning. If Mr. Johnson so much as took one step closer—

"Marissa," Fable's voice floated softly from behind Blaze, interrupting his thoughts. "If you would, please call the police. It seems Mr. Johnson may need to be detained until he can get control over himself. Let them know we have an aggressive man here who is scaring our clients, and refuses to leave." Blaze marveled at how calm and cold Fable sounded. As if this were a regular occurrence, and only a passing inconvenience. Perhaps it was, Blaze didn't know that much about the life of a veterinarian. If Mr. Johnson was anything to go by, it seemed Fable put up with plenty of abuse.

"You wouldn't," Mr. Johnson hissed.

Fable stepped from behind Blaze to look the furious

man in the face. "I assure you, Mr. Johnson, I would. While I care deeply for Gidget's health and safety, I cannot put your wants above the needs of my other patients," his words remained deadly calm, only a soft edge that hinted at his underlying anger.

"I won't be back," Mr. Johnson threatened weakly, his feet betraying him as he backed away.

"I think that would be best," Fable agreed reasonably with a nod. "If you cannot behave respectfully towards myself, my staff, or my other patients, it may be best if you find another vet."

"I'll leave a bad review!" The man's back was against the glass door now, but he stilled to wag his finger threateningly at Fable.

"If the mood strikes you, feel free." Fable shrugged.

"I'll tell everyone," Mr. Johnson declared, just before he slipped out of the door.

The door shut, and Fable's shoulders sagged a moment later. "Marissa, I'll be in my office. Can you hold off my next patient for just a few minutes? I think I need to breathe," he whispered to Purple-hair.

The girl's eyes flicked from the vet to Blaze, then back again. "You next patient is Mr. Ender," she whispered back as if perhaps Blaze—who was standing right there—wouldn't hear.

Blaze frowned, shaking out one clenched fist to dispel the residual heat lingering there. "You take a break, I've got time." He shrugged, then scooped up the dog carrier and returned to his place leaning against the wall, to wait. Although he couldn't see it, Blaze could feel the eyes of the entire room on him. He ducked his head back to his phone, vowing to ignore everyone until they called him.

Instead of watching the time, he texted Eero back.

Blaze 3:00PM
> Wtf are you talking about?

Eero 3:00PM
> You know, with the mage.

Blaze 3:01PM
> It's a vet appointment. Not a date you dipshit

Eero 3:02PM
> Whatever you say fire crotch

Blaze 3:03PM
> I told you to stop f-ing calling me that shit for brains!

Eero 3:04PM
> Love you tooooooo <3

With a growl, Blaze decided not to dignify that with a response. Instead, he settled in to scroll through the latest headlines. It didn't feel like long at all, before a smiling blond vet-tech was at his side. "Mr. Ender? Doctor A is ready to see you now, we'll be in exam room C. You can follow me." Then, the young man turned, expecting Blaze to follow.

Blaze set the carrier carefully on the metal table in the exam room, and pulled out the little dog. "It's all right, Baku," he soothed softly, trying to quell the pup's shivering.

"Oh, is this Bakugo? He's so cute!" The vet-tech giggled, leaning in to get a better look at the dog while still giving him his space. "I read the chart. Doctor A says you saved him from a fire?"

Blaze shrugged, stroking the dog until he finally seemed to settle down.

"That's sweet." The young man grinned brightly up at him, almost blindingly.

"Whatever. Where is Doctor Alperen?" Blaze had no desire to stand there and shoot the shit with this guy. *Why is everyone in this office so damn chipper,* he wondered. *Is it something in the water?*

"He'll be right in. We're just going to take Bakugo's temperature and get everything set up for his vaccinations. Aren't we little buddy?" The guy cooed soothingly to the dog, who leaned into his gentle touches. *Traitor,* Blaze thought irritably.

"It won't hurt him, will it?" Blaze couldn't help the worry he felt welling up in his chest. The little dog had just come into his own, Blaze didn't want him cowering under the damn futon again.

"It'll be a little pinch, but Doctor A is good at these things," the tech assured him. Bakugo growled when the tech took his temperature, but they kept him relaxed enough to get all the information needed for his chart. "Doctor A will be in soon," the tech chirped, scribbling everything down, and then skipping out.

Blaze tugged the chair from the corner and sat down, so he and the little dog were closer to eye level. Bakugo licked his nose happily, and Blaze sighed, scratching behind one scruffy brown ear. "We're going to kick Eero's ass when we see him later. Aren't we?"

Bakugo yipped, wagging his stubby tail.

"No. You're just threatening enough, I think he'll be terrified."

"Mr. Ender," Fable breathed as he stepped into the room, his eyes firmly on the chart. Blaze's eyes flicked over him, taking in the absence of the white lab coat he'd been wearing before, the short-sleeved scrubs, and the rapidly forming bruise on his elbow. *Shit, I didn't think he'd hit it that hard*, Blaze winced as he looked at the injury. Blaze frowned, forcing his eyes away from the blossoming bruise. It was none of his business. So, he ducked his head back to the dog instead. "I see Bakugo is doing much better."

"Yeah, he's been eating and drinking fine. We stopped with the wet food, and he's on straight kibble now," there was a note of pride in Blaze's tone. He'd helped Bakugo get better. He'd done that.

"Has he been using the bathroom outside?" Fable's pen scratched against the paper as he took notes.

"Not yet, I'm not really sure how to initiate that," Blaze admitted with a shrug. The pride slipped away, and he looked up from the dog, finally, to give Fable an uncertain expression. He felt lost, he'd never taken care of anyone, or anything, other than himself. What if he messed this up? He'd been doing all right so far, but there was still so much more he didn't know.

Fable's brow wrinkled in thought. Then he turned to grab another pamphlet. "This should help."

Blaze took it, amber eyes flicking over the 'potty training' pamphlet. "Right, thanks."

"No need to thank me, that's part of my job." Fable had turned to prep the vaccinations. Blaze stared at his back, wondering if it really were his job to be this helpful. House calls seemed well outside the purview of a typical vet, but he decided not to ask. "Hold this," Fable instructed when he turned back, holding out a few treats to Blaze. The vet seemed to note the confusion on Blaze's face, and said by way of explanation, "to keep him distracted while I do his shots. Let him lick them, but don't let him eat them yet."

With a nod, Blaze tucked the treats into his fingers just far enough out of reach that Bakugo couldn't eat them. Fable made quick work of giving the dog his shots while he snuffled against Blaze's closed fingers. When he finished, Fable gave Blaze a quick nod, and Blaze opened his hand for Bakugo to snarf down the treats, tail wagging.

"You, um... you handled yourself really well back there with that asshole," Blaze mumbled. *Why did I say that*, he asked himself. Strawberry blond brows knit together as he realized the words had left him unbidden.

Fable's blue and green eyes flicked up from the chart where he was jotting down notes to give Blaze a quizzical look. "I'm used to people like that." He shrugged.

"You get a lot of dickheads in here who don't know how to act?" Why did he care? He didn't care. Did he care? *I'm just curious*, he told himself. He'd never gotten to know the mage in his first life, and now that they were at least on speaking terms, Blaze was interested. What made a person like Fable chase down a dragon?

"Yes, and no." Fable shrugged again. He ducked his head back to his notes.

"What the hell does that mean?"

Fable snorted, looking up from the papers again. "It means yes, we have a lot of crappy people who come through here. People who don't know enough to get their heads out of their own asses and take my advice. We also have a lot of great pet owners too. People like you, who truly care, and want to do whatever they can for their animal."

Was Blaze blushing under the praise? He hoped to hell not! But his cheeks definitely felt warmer than they ought to. *Shit.* "Right," he grunted finally.

If he was blushing, Fable didn't seem to notice. "Bakugo is good to go. It sounds like his lungs are all cleared up, and his eyes have sorted themselves out nicely. Unless something comes up, we shouldn't need to see him in here again until his next round of shots. Marissa can get you all set up with an appointment for those at the front desk."

"Uh, thanks." Blaze all but stumbled over the words, settling Bakugo back into the carrier.

"Of course. It was nice seeing you, Mr. Ender." Fable turned to fix him with a dazzling smile. "This way." He led Blaze back to the front desk. "And just as before," Fable continued, voice pitched low, the tone sending a strange flutter through Blaze's stomach. "Please, don't hesitate to call should you need anything."

Blaze nodded dumbly.

"Marissa." Fable fixed Purple-hair with that bright smile. "Mr. Ender needs to make a follow-up visit for Bakugo's next round of shots. And see if you can dig up more pamphlets on house training for him? We only had the one back in the exam room." Then he turned on his heel and left Blaze in the capable hands of Purple-hair. Blaze shook himself to loosen the strange, fuzzy feeling gripping his mind so he could focus on what Purple-hair was saying.

FIVE

Fable sat at his desk, typing in some information from a file one-handed as he munched on his lunch. Movement out of the corner of his eye drew his attention to Aura —poking her head into the office. He groaned. "What do you want, Aura?"

"I heard you had an encounter with our favorite white knight earlier," she teased, trotting over to lean onto his desk. "Tell me everything."

"In-house gossip is gross," was his only response as he stuffed a too-big bite of romaine lettuce into his mouth. He had absolutely no desire to discuss Blaze Ender with anyone. The conundrum that was Blaze Ender was far from his mind now, and he'd like it to stay that way. Thank you very much. Judging by the glint in her eye, Aura would have none of it. "And when did we start calling him a white knight?"

"When he physically put himself between you and a client who was getting out of hand," Aura huffed, flopping onto the desk face-first to smack her head lightly against the pressboard. She sat there, with her forehead pressed to the desk, waiting on him to continue. Fable rolled his eyes at her theatrics, but kept eating his salad without a word. "Tell me, or I'm telling your mama you still aren't dating anyone," her words came out muffled by the desk, but Fable heard the threat just fine.

Fable shrugged. "Go ahead, she probably already knows."

Aura lifted her head, a devious smirk stretching her lips. "Tell me, or I'm telling your mama you're taking extra shifts to avoid the people who *have* asked you out."

Fable blinked mismatched eyes at her, then scowled. His mother was primarily worried about two things—him never finding love and dying alone, and him working himself too hard. "You're evil, do you know that?"

"So I'm told." She grinned, standing up finally.

"Seriously. Satan incarnate."

"Yeah, yeah, yeah. Tell me everything," she demanded, snatching a cucumber from his salad. It crunched loudly as she sat on the corner of his desk to listen.

ANOTHER NIGHT, another nightmare. Fable drifted in and out of sleep. Behind his lids, flashes of a scowling face lashed out towards him, causing his dream-self to stumble back. Then a carriage careened towards him, and just before it collided, he jerked awake. Fable sat up, clutching his chest to calm his racing heart.

Jiji looked up from where he perched on Fable's stomach to glare at him. The dogs to either side of him slept on, unbothered by their human's distress. With a deep breath, Fable forced himself to calm down.

"I know Jiji. I'm having a lot of these lately," he huffed,

and flopped back down into bed, forcing his eyes shut. If he could just get himself back to sleep—a set of snarling amber eyes jerked his eyes open again. "This won't work. What time is it?"

Fable rolled over, grabbed his phone, and groaned. Too early, it was much too early for this nonsense. Still, he dragged himself to his feet and got dressed for a run. If he couldn't sleep, at least he could work off some nervous energy. After all, he was always telling Aura and his doctor that he'd exercise more—now seemed as good a time as any to make good on those promises.

The sound of his soft footfalls quieted his mind little by little. By the time he'd made his way to work after dealing with the dogs and making breakfast, he felt calmer than he had in a long time. Maybe there was something to this running thing other than just the health benefits. Karen looked up from where she was working on a crossword puzzle to eye him. "You're early, Doctor A."

Fable shrugged, scrubbing a hand through his still damp curls. "Yeah, well, I figured Aura could use the help since she's got so many patients this morning."

Karen's eyes narrowed on him suspiciously, but then she shrugged. The morning carried on as it usually did after that. Fable met with his few scheduled patients, but somehow Aura had overbooked herself again, and at some point, he found himself in an exam room with one of her patients.

"I'm so sorry, Doctor Guthrie won't be able to see you today. I'm Doctor Alperen, what can I help you with?" He looked up from the chart to meet a pair of golden eyes set into a beautiful smiling face with a strong jaw and long red hair. "Mister Heathcliff?"

"Oh, no, Heathcliff is my bird." They laughed, pointing

to the little love bird perched happily on their shoulder. "I'm Gwydion." They held out one perfectly manicured hand.

"Mist—Miss," Fable stumbled, not wanting to say the wrong thing as he reached over to shake their hand. "I'm sorry, what do you prefer?"

"Just Gwydion will be fine. Let's not be so formal, Doctor Alperen," they purred softly, giving Fable's hand a firm shake before pulling their hand back.

"Right, of course, Gwydion." Fable smiled, a flush staining his freckled cheeks. "You can call me Fable."

Full lips split into a toothy smile, and Gwydion nodded happily. "It's a pleasure to meet you, Fable."

Mismatched eyes flicked back down to the chart in his hands. "So, you just brought in Heathcliff for a checkup, is that right? Doctor Guthrie saw him about a year ago, and he seemed in fine shape then." He muttered dates, and numbers, and facts about birds to himself as he read over the file. Gwydion watched him until he finished and then met his eyes with a smile.

"Yes, nothing has changed. I just like to be sure he's all right. Plus, Aura told me a cute new vet was working here, and I had to see for myself," Gwydion cooed, a mischievous light twinkling in their golden eyes.

The flush on Fable's cheeks increased, and he cleared his throat awkwardly. "She would say that," he grumbled, shaking his head. He wondered idly how many other patients Aura had said that to, and then thought it better not to find out. "All right Heathcliff, let's get a look at you, shall we?" He held up a hand and the bird chirped delightedly, hopping over to the new perch. "You're a friendly little guy, aren't you?"

"Oh yes, he's quite the friendliest." Gwydion clucked at the little bird who fluttered his wings bashfully.

Fable went through the motions of the checkup, smiling softly when the bird pressed his head into Fable's jaw while he jotted down some notes. Heathcliff seemed in the peak of health, unlike some other birds Fable had treated. He lifted his hand to yawn into the back of it on reflex as he worked.

"I'm sorry, are we keeping you up?" Gwydion teased gently, a smirk tugging up the corner of their red-painted lips.

Fable chuckled. "No, I just haven't been sleeping well recently." He wasn't sure why he had admitted it, but there was something about the person before him that was distinctly disarming. Gwydion looked like the type of person who Fable wouldn't mind going out for drinks with to blow off some steam. No wonder Aura liked them so much.

"Oh no. Tell Auntie Gwydion what's wrong." Gwydion's lips settled into a soft pout. "Maybe I can help?"

"Unless you have a cure for nightmares, I doubt it. But thanks for the offer." Fable smiled, shaking his head.

"No, I'm afraid not." Gwydion frowned, their hands stroking the little bird on the table absently. "Maybe if you talked about them, they would sort themselves out?" Again, there was a glint in Gwydion's eyes; this time it was something Fable couldn't quite place. It wasn't malicious. If Fable had to venture a guess, he'd say it was 'all knowing.' Which seemed strange, for he'd never met Gwydion before. Still, just as there had been with Blaze, there was something familiar about Gwydion's golden eyes niggling at the back of Fable's mind.

"It's really not important. Thank you for your concern,"

Fable murmured, hoping to put an end to the conversation there. He shifted his weight from one foot to the other as he felt Gwydion's eyes flicking over him, searching for something.

"You know they say that sometimes dreams show us our past lives," Gwydion ventured, their eyes landing finally on Fable's face, but Fable studiously avoided their gaze. "That it's us trying to remember all those lives."

"Well, I highly doubt a dragon attacked me in a past life. That seems ridiculous," Fable laughed tiredly, hoping the subject would drop. He didn't believe in dream journals, or dream science, and he definitely didn't believe in reincarnation, or dragons. "Either way, it looks like Heathcliff is good to go. You can settle up with Karen at the front desk."

Gwydion looked hurt at being dismissed, but instead of saying so, they reached into their purse and pulled out a business card. "If you want to talk, I work weird hours," they offered sincerely. "I'm always up when everyone else is asleep."

"I, uh, thanks," Fable said, taking the card. It probably wasn't professional to take a client's number just because one might need someone to talk to. Still, Fable tried not to overthink it. He probably wouldn't even call, right?

"Of course, darling, any friend of Aura's is a friend of mine." They winked, and then loaded the little love bird into a small carrier, before trotting out.

Fable shook his head, tucking the card into his pocket. "People in the city sure are friendly," he muttered to himself.

FABLE WAS sure that since he'd cleared Bakugo, he wouldn't be seeing Mr. Ender again anytime soon. He was fine with that, he really was. He had too much else to worry about to be distracted by a handsome firefighter who seemed to have a soft spot for distressed animals, a colorful vocabulary, and a temper to match. Maybe Blaze would even find a different vet now that the dog was healthy. That would be fine. Fable hadn't come to New York looking for a boyfriend, he had come here to escape the suffocating air of his small town. There was so much else to do besides dating.

"We should go out tonight," Aura insisted as she grabbed her purse. "Come on, I heard there is a new bar in Brooklyn that everyone is raving about."

Fable frowned. "I don't know Aura. You know that's not really my thing—anymore." He grumbled the word 'anymore' self-consciously. There had been a time when he and his friends would hit the bars and not get home until the wee hours of the morning. When he'd crawl into bed and sleep through the following day's hangover. But that was behind him now. He had a much healthier respect for alcohol, and his own personal limitations these days.

"I know, but you haven't been out since you moved to the city." She pouted up at him, big brown eyes going impossibly wider in a puppy dog expression she knew he struggled to say 'no' to.

"That's not true, I went out that first weekend I was here, remember? I had to carry you to the subway station." He smirked as they stepped out of the building.

"Fable, that was months ago!" A couple on the sidewalk across the street looked over at Aura's exclamation, and Fable rolled his eyes. "You don't date, you don't go out. Why did you even bother moving to the city in the first place?"

"The fresh air," Fable teased and set Aura into a fit of

giggles. "I'll make you a deal, we have Sunday off, let's go out Saturday night?"

Aura narrowed her eyes on him for a moment, then nodded. She held her hand out to shake. "Shake on it, or I won't believe you mean it."

He laughed and shook her hand roughly. "There, now, can I go home?"

"I guuuuueeeess," she drawled, drawing the word out dramatically. But then she skipped off toward her apartment with no more fuss.

FABLE MUST HAVE DOZED off at some point. For when the buzzing of his phone woke him, he was on the couch where he'd been curled up with the dogs, trying to watch a movie to settle his rattled nerves. He swiped drool from his cheek before checking his phone. It took a moment for the contact name to register before he picked it up. "Mr. Ender? What can I do for you?" his words were fuzzy, and sleep addled, but he tried to put a smile behind them.

"He doesn't like the harness," Blaze growled irritably. "The girl at the pet store said it wouldn't be a problem, but every time I get near him with the damn thing, he snarls at me."

"This is really a training issue, not a health issue, Mr. Ender," Fable offered with an amused smirk tugging at his lips. "I can put you in touch with a trainer."

"How the hell am I supposed to take him outside if I can't put the harness on him? I just want him to go—" Blaze stopped talking, his voice muffled as it sounded like he pulled the phone away from his ear to snap at the dog. "Oi! Don't do that! Don't piss there!"

Fable couldn't help himself; he was laughing at the other man's expense before he realized he'd started. It was probably because he was sleep-deprived. Definitely. Otherwise, he wouldn't be lifting himself from the couch and gathering his things together to head right over. His judgment was clearly impaired. "Have you tried not growling back at him?"

"No shit," Blaze huffed. "Look, if I can just get the harness on him then we can get this shit show over with. Do you have a minute?"

"I should really start charging you for these late-night visits," Fable teased as he slipped into a pair of shoes.

"It's not even that late! It's barely nine o'clock. What? Is your bedtime at like six or something? Are you an old lady, and you just didn't tell me?" Blaze snarked. But Fable was almost sure he could hear the other man smiling.

"I'll be over in a bit. Just try to keep your shit together, Mr. Ender." A smirk tugged at Fable's lips as he slung his messenger bag over his shoulder.

"What the fu—" Blaze shouted into the phone, but Fable promptly hung up before he could finish.

Grabbing a cab was easier this time; he sat in silence on the way to the familiar building. When he reached Blaze's floor, Blaze was waiting for him, leaning against the door frame. "Mr. Ender," Fable greeted, still smirking to himself in wry amusement.

"Do you always hang up on patients?" Blaze bared sharp canines in obvious irritation.

The smirk slipped from Fable's lips. An image flashed in his mind of a scaly red face with a mouth full of teeth, but he shook it away. "When they're acting like petulant children, yes. Now, where's Bakugo?"

Blaze didn't say anything else. He stepped aside to let

Fable inside where the little dog was sitting on the floor, snarling at the discarded harness.

A soft laugh burbled up in Fable's throat, drawing the dog's attention. Bakugo stopped snarling to blink up at the vet. "Hi there, Bakugo," he cooed softly, kneeling down onto the floor to be at the dog's level. "Let's see what's the matter with this harness, huh?" Fable scooped up the offending collar, but the dog didn't react.

"You little shit," Blaze groused, pointing an accusing finger at the dog. "Every time I pick it up you growl at me!"

"Are you nervous, Mr. Ender?" Fable asked offhandedly, luring the dog closer with a treat from his pocket.

"What? No, I'm not—" Blaze's eyes widened as the dog calmly stepped into the harness for Fable. Once clipped, Fable gave him an affectionate scratch under the chin. "How did you do that? Are you some kind of witch?"

"Your nervous energy was making him nervous," Fable stated with a shrug. "You've just got to be calm, and he'll know everything will be all right. Dogs are excellent at reading people." Fable's face scrunched up in thought as he hooked the leash to the dog's harness. He wondered if Blaze had a calm bone in his body. The other man seemed to jump from emotion to emotion, like a child playing hopscotch.

"Right. Whatever," Blaze huffed, petulantly. "Can we take the little shit for a walk now?"

Fable blinked for a moment in confusion. Was Blaze expecting him to go on a walk with him? That was— weird. He'd assumed once he'd gotten Bakugo in the harness that he could go back home. "I should really head—"

"Where? Back to your knitting, Grandma?" Blaze teased, sharp teeth exposed in a cross between a snarl and a smirk. Fable wasn't sure which was winning, but he decided it was best not to think too much on it.

"Actually, I was going home to bed," Fable finished with a sigh. He thought to tell Blaze that he'd had trouble sleeping lately, but decided against it. He'd already burdened one client with his own issues that day and wouldn't do so with another. Besides, whatever this was that was forming between them seemed fragile somehow. Like if he weighed it down with his issues it may crumble under the weight.

Blaze quirked a brow at him, but headed out into the hall with the little dog scooped up in his arms. "So, you really are an old lady," Blaze muttered with a smirk. He jammed a button for the elevator, and stood back to wait. "Didn't you just move here, or something? People who just moved into the city are usually all gung-ho to bar hop every night. Or would that interfere with your book club? What are you guys reading this week? Another bodice ripper?"

Fable rolled his eyes, biting back a soft laugh at the ribbing. "I'll have you know, Mr. Ender, we prefer cozy mysteries." This comment earned him a surprised chuckle from Blaze, which Fable would never admit was kind of cute. "No, but in all seriousness, I'm going out this weekend with Aura. So there." He resisted the urge to stick his tongue out at the other man. He was an adult, after all.

"Blaze," Blaze grunted, climbing onto the elevator when the doors opened.

Fable stood for a moment, blinking in confusion as a blush settled into his cheeks. "What?"

"No more of this, Mr. Ender shit. It's just Blaze," Blaze said. His arm held the door open for Fable as he watched him expectantly. "You getting in or what?"

"Oh, uh, right," Fable yelped, climbing into the elevator

beside him. They rode down to the main floor in silence, Fable shifting awkwardly on his feet as Blaze stared straight ahead of them. Once out on the sidewalk, Fable took a deep breath and nodded to himself. "You can call me Fable," he insisted, then, feeling heat crawl up his neck he added, "Since we're not doing the formality thing anymore. There isn't any point in calling me Doctor Alperen," he clarified.

Blaze quirked a brow, but said nothing as he strode over to a small patch of grass across the street and set down the little dog. "Go potty," he commanded, and the dog just looked at him, confused.

Fable bit back a laugh, shaking his head. "He probably doesn't know what that means."

"What do you mean he doesn't know what it means? That's what that shitty pamphlet you gave me said to say." Blaze sounded irritated, but nowhere near as angry as Fable had heard him in the past.

"I mean, it's not a command he knows yet. You'll have to teach it to him. So, when he goes to the bathroom, praise him and say it. Then he'll start associating those words with the action." Fable smiled more, watching Bakugo for a moment. The dog snuffled softly as he sniffed the grass. Then, seeming to find a spot he liked, he hiked up one leg and peed. "Like this," Fable offered, and then squatted down to the little dog once he was finished. "That's a good boy, Bakugo. Good boy. Go potty. Good boy going potties outside," he cooed, scratching the dog behind the ear. Bakugo's nubby tail wagged quickly in excitement.

Blaze stood watching them both with an unreadable expression before asking, "Do I have to do that every damn time?"

"Yup, every damn time." Fable smirked as he stood. "And you should probably bring him out every hour or so while he's awake until he gets the message that this is where he goes, not inside."

Blaze heaved a heavy sigh but nodded. "And how do I get him to do the other one?"

"I usually use the word poops." Fable shrugged. "He won't do that every time, though. But eventually you'll see a schedule of when he does. My dogs go once in the morning, right after dinner, and then usually right before bed."

"And the—" Blaze gestured with a wrinkle of his angular nose.

"Positive reinforcement? Yeah, you do it when they do that too." Fable couldn't help but chuckle. There was something endearingly hopeless about Blaze in this moment. It was like he wanted to do his best, but just didn't know how. Nor did he seem to know how to ask for help. Fable made a mental note to never share this with Aura, she'd be a puddle. "Has he had his dinner already?"

Blaze nodded.

"Then let's give him a minute. Maybe he'll do poops too. Did you bring any bags?"

"What?"

Fable snorted, digging around in his messenger bag before producing a roll of lightly scented bags. "Of course, you didn't. You can't just leave it on the side of the street like an asshole." He dropped the roll into Blaze's hand. The other man's amber eyes narrowed on them for a moment before he nodded in understanding. "Oh, there he goes, your turn." Fable grinned down at the little dog who had squatted in the grass.

"My turn?" Blaze asked, confusion drawing his strawberry blond brows together.

"Yes, your turn. Praise him, tell him he did a good job," Fable encouraged.

Blaze lowered awkwardly down towards the ground, holding out a hand to pet the dog when it trotted over to him. "That's a good job. Good boy, Baku." He looked up when Fable nudged him with his foot and frowned. "Going poops outside," he muttered, his shoulders hunching. Bakugo yipped happily at the encouragement. "And I do this again in an hour?"

"Yup, until he gets the hang of it. Eventually he'll tell you when he needs to go out."

"This is so weird," Blaze mumbled, scooping up the little dog again before cleaning up his mess, and throwing it into a nearby bin.

"Such is the life of a pet owner," Fable snickered.

"Uh, right, well, thanks Doc," Blaze offered, scratching at his jaw a little.

"No problem! Happy to help. Now, if you don't mind, I'm going to get back to that scarf I was knitting." Fable winked, spun on his heel, and trotted away to hail a cab.

SIX

Blaze wasn't sure what it was about seeing Fable in his element—helping animals—but it had stuck with him. He found himself wondering if Fable were always so relaxed, or if it were just with animals. Had he been that way even in the beginning?

The simple answer was yes, he had been. Alone in his caves, Blaze had watched the little fishing village where Fable had grown up all of his life. And he'd seen the head of brown curls, face splattered in too many freckles, and eyes shining too brightly enough times to know. Even then, Fable was most in his element when he was helping someone else. It was as if there was a spring wound too tight in Fable's chest, and it only eased when Fable took his attention away from himself, and focused it on someone else. Blaze had seen it.

A towel smacked him in the face, ripping Blaze from his thoughts. "What the—" he growled, eyes narrowing on Eero who stood behind the punching bag, smirking.

"You back, space cadet?"

"Space cadet? Who says that anymore? Did you get

stuck in the nineties?" Blaze snorted, tossing the towel over his shoulder.

Eero shrugged. "You were the one zoning out, dude. I've been sitting here talking for a straight two minutes, and nothing."

Had it been that long? Blaze shook himself internally. *Get a hold of yourself, man.* He rolled his shoulders, stretching one arm across his chest. "So? What d'you want?"

"I said, how's Bakugo doing?" Eero huffed, crossing his arms over his chest, but his expression didn't look near as put out as he was aiming for. If anything, he looked amused. *Great.*

"Oh, he's good. We're working on the house-training thing. I had Fable give me a rundown on how to handle it." The words left his mouth before he thought better of them, and Blaze knew he'd said the wrong thing when Eero's red brows shot up. "What?"

"You're on a first-name basis with Doctor Alperen?"

"Yeah." Blaze shrugged. He met Eero's eyes head-on, unwilling to back down now. "What of it?" Blaze asked, trying not to sound defensive.

"When did that happen?" Eero smirked.

"That's none of your damn business, elf boy."

"I am a dryad, not an elf," Eero grumbled, falling into a sulk. Blaze smirked, pleased that he seemed to have derailed the conversation, and went back to punching the bag. It didn't take Eero long to regain himself, though. He moved to keep the bag from swaying and eyed Blaze knowingly from behind it. That damn asshole looked so smug. "Been seeing a lot of him, have you?"

Blaze didn't meet his eyes and didn't respond. He wondered how long Eero would needle him about this, and if he could hold out. Maybe he should just punch him and get this whole thing over with. Then they wouldn't have to play this game of back and forth.

"I thought Bakugo had only been to the vet twice since the fire." Eero's voice was soft, leading. The kind of voice humans would follow into a fairy circle and get trapped with.

Blaze ignored it.

"You know, I was talking to Aura, she said you stepped in the middle of what could have been a nasty throw down at the vet the other day."

"Since when are you and Doctor Guthrie on a first name basis?" Blaze countered, a smirk of his own splitting his lips. It wasn't much of a secret that Eero had been drooling over her since he'd first taken his lizard there, but Blaze'd be damned if he'd be the only one uncomfortable in this conversation.

Eero flushed, but pressed on. "She's been Cami's vet for like three years, of course we are."

Blaze quirked a brow, eyeing him blandly. "The guy shoved him. Nothing more to it. You would have done the same thing."

"Riiiight," Eero said, drawing the word out as if he didn't quite believe it.

"You got something to say? Say it. Stop with the bull-shit." Blaze glowered, landing a hard punch to the bag that made Eero stumble backward.

"Oh, it's nothing." Eero's words were soft, but they lingered. It made Blaze want to sock Eero in the gut and push all the air from his lungs. They'd see if he could manage that smug ass tone when he couldn't breathe. "I just heard from a little birdie that Fable gave you his personal number."

Blaze clenched his teeth in annoyance, squeezing his

eyes shut. Eero wouldn't let this go, and of course Aura had run her mouth. Blaze didn't know her, but she looked the type to never let a good bit of gossip pass her by. Damn busy bodies. "Yeah, so I could call him if I had questions about Bakugo. Which I did. Twice," Blaze answered flatly. "We done?"

"I see." Eero lifted a hand to scratch at his chin, a look of mischief in his eyes. That was an expression no one ever wanted to see on a fae's face.

"What are you up to?"

"Nothing." Eero shrugged, heading over to one of the treadmills lining the wall. "Nothing at all."

Blaze glared after him, but decided not to push it. He wanted to call bullshit, but it wasn't worth it. He didn't care. He did not give a flying shit what Eero was up to. Let the stupid dryad be all mysterious and annoying, Blaze had more important things to worry about.

HE DOESN'T KNOW how Eero did it, because he definitely said 'no.' He remembered saying 'no.' Right? And yet, there he was, waiting in line for a club tucked into a back alley near Chelsea. A bead of sweat trickled down underneath the back of his black v-neck. "You need to look nice," Eero had told him when he'd first opened the door wearing a ragged, too-thin, white t-shirt, and a pair of baggy gym shorts. So, he'd changed, but now Blaze was regretting it. Even with the sun having set hours before, the New York heat was stifling, and he doubted the inside of the club would be any cooler. Not with how many bodies were currently pressing to get inside.

Eero's phone buzzed, and he pulled it out to check a text he'd gotten before muttering, "Oh, they're almost here."

"They?" Blaze asked, his jaw ticking in annoyance. He should have known this was some kind of setup. With Eero, it always was. It was the fae blood in him. They couldn't help but be sneaky bastards. "I thought it was just going to be us?"

"You don't go to a club with just two people Blaze," Eero snorted, as if Blaze ought to know better than that. "Especially two guys. Nobody does that."

"How should I know? I don't go to clubs at all," Blaze growled, his eyes narrowing as his palms heated in irritation. All he could hope was that Eero had invited some of the guys from the station and hadn't gotten it into his pretty little head to play matchmaker. "Who did you invite, anyway?" Not that he cared. Right?

Eero shrugged, ducking his head to look at his phone again. "Don't worry about it."

"Don't worry about it?" Blaze felt his temper slipping. His palms grew hot again, and he was half tempted to grab the phone from Eero's hands and reduce it to ash. A sinking feeling settled into the pit of his stomach as the memory of that smug expression Eero had been wearing not but a day ago flashed through his mind. "What did you do?" he hissed.

Instead of answering, Eero looked up from his phone to smile down the street. He lifted his hand to beckon whoever he'd seen in their direction. "Aura! Fable! We're over here!"

"I'm going to kill you," Blaze threatened under his breath.

"Get in line," Eero responded through smiling teeth with a shrug—completely unfazed.

"Oh great, you guys are almost in!" Aura cheered as she

bounced up to them in a short, sparkly, halter dress. It made Blaze feel underdressed, but he decided that it didn't matter. He wasn't there to impress anyone, anyway. "Sorry we're late, getting a cab over was hell." She slipped beneath the velvet rope to stand between the two men.

"Hey! No cutting!" some girl—who couldn't be much older than twenty-two in a pair of heels that made her wobble—whined.

Aura pointedly ignored her. "I'm Aura." She held her hand out to Blaze. "You must be Blaze. I've heard so much about you." Her smile was too big for her face, forcing her eyes to squint to make room for it. Within those squinted depths was a teasing light that Blaze decided he didn't much care for. It reminded him of Eero and his plotting.

Blaze blinked at her for a moment, his eyes flicking to Fable—who had ducked under the rope to stand behind Eero. The vet was wearing a fitted green button-up with the sleeves rolled up to his elbows to show off toned, freckled forearms sporting bruises in varying degrees of healing. He looked uncomfortable; Blaze noted with irritation. Well, at least he wasn't the only one.

"Only the good things, I promise," Eero assured with a grin, and a soft chuckle.

"Nice to meet you," Blaze muttered in a detached, polite tone. Then he shook her hand, perhaps a little harder than was necessary.

"And who's your cute friend?" Eero asked as if he hadn't just shouted Fable's name for the world to hear. The teasing light from Aura's eyes seemed to have transferred to his. Everyone turned to Fable, who flushed brightly under his freckles at the sudden attention.

"Oh, uh, Fable." Fable held his hand out to Eero. "A pleasure."

"And this is my friend," Eero started and then laughed. "Oh, that's right, you already know each other, don't you?" A coy smile had split Eero's lips, but he and Aura shared a look as if they were both in on some inside joke. Blaze would definitely kill him later.

"Line's moving!" someone shouted from the back.

Aura trotted over to hook her arm through Fable's and led him ahead of the other two. Just far enough away for Blaze to snarl at Eero out of earshot. "If you wanted a wingman, you could have just asked."

"How are you so sure *I'm* not the wingman here?" Eero teased.

"You're dead to me."

"You say that at least once a week." Eero laughed and turned to the bouncer to present his ID.

Inside the club, the music was so loud Blaze could feel his teeth rattling. "I wanna dance," Aura announced, looking to Eero expectantly. She still had a death grip on Fable's arm, and was half dragging him to the dance floor.

"How about I get us some drinks?" Fable offered, peeling her hand off his arm carefully.

"What? Don't you want to dance?" Eero asked, his brows raised to disappear into his bangs.

"Oh, Fable hates dancing," Aura sniggered. She grabbed Eero's wrist, and started tugging him instead. "Come on."

"I'll go with him," Blaze added, ignoring the knowing look Eero shot him. "What do you want?"

Eero laughed softly, shaking his head. "Baby, you know what I like." Then he winked, looped his arm around Aura's waist, and lead her towards the crowded dance floor.

"Stick close," Blaze ordered. Fable nodded as they both turned to make a beeline through the crowd towards the bar. A hand caught at the back of Blaze's shirt, and he looked down to see Fable gripping it as they pushed their way through. Once there, Blaze shouldered a few people aside and reached back to tug the shorter man in front of him—pointedly ignoring the little *eep* Fable made. It was just easier with the place being so packed, he told himself as his hands gripped the bar on either side of Fable. "Oi!" he shouted to the bartender, flagging her down.

The bartender held up a finger to show that she'd be a minute.

"So," Fable started awkwardly. "You and Eero are..." He let the words drift off in question.

Blaze snorted, rolling his eyes. People always thought he and Eero were together, or brothers. He wondered which Fable assumed. "We work at the station together. Eero says I'm hist best friend."

Fable laughed—a loud, short snort of laughter. Blaze blinked down at him. The vet had a nice laugh. He didn't think he'd ever heard it before, had he? Fable shook his head full of brunette curls before explaining. "Sorry. I just—so if you're his best friend, then he's your? What?"

"Long time annoyance," Blaze answered, a little smile tugging at the corner of his lips.

"I see." Fable chortled with barely restrained mirth. Blaze opened his mouth to respond, but that's when the bartender graced them with her presence. Fable turned his attention to her so he could order. "I need a vodka soda and a white wine spritzer."

"And I need a gin and tonic and a maple cinnamon whiskey sour." The bartender tilted her head, and Blaze scowled. "Look it up," he grumbled dismissively. Fable was laughing again when Blaze ducked his head to look down at him. His freckled cheeks scrunched in mirth; it was almost cute. "What?"

"Maybe you should carry the recipe for whatever that is in on a card," Fable teased.

"I'm not a tool," Blaze huffed.

"Yeah, okay." Fable continued to snicker. "You sound kind of like a tool when you order something the bartender doesn't recognize."

"Whatever," Blaze grunted. They lapsed into silence while they waited for their drinks.

When the bartender slid Blaze's drink to him, Fable announced, "Okay, I need to try that. Whatever it is." Then he grabbed the drink before Blaze could take it, and took a quick, careful sip. He grimaced, coughing a little. "Ewwwww, it burns!"

Blaze snickered, snatching his drink back. "Big baby, that'll teach you to take someone else's drink," he grumbled as he took a sip. "Come on, let's find those two before they slink off to a corner somewhere." Fable followed closely behind as Blaze's eyes swept the dance floor till he found their friends.

FABLE DID NOT LIKE to dance—just as Aura had said. And not only did he not like it, but he also wasn't very good at it, Blaze quickly learned. He was a limp noodle who seemed like his brain wasn't attached to his body half the time, and struggled to even do the Cabbage Patch. Blaze didn't use the word adorable lightly, but Fable's 'slick moves'—Fable's words, not anyone else's—seemed to be just that.

At some point, his arm swung a little too wild, nearly knocking Aura's drink out of her hand. "Woah there, killer, time for you to take a breather." She giggled lightly, pointing over to an empty booth. "I'll grab you a water and be right over."

Fable nodded slowly, and turned towards the seats.

"Blaze can get him some water," Eero volunteered.

"What the—" a sharp elbow to the ribs stopped the words as they left Blaze's lips. Blaze shot Eero a scowl, and the other man returned it with a pleading look. "Right, I've got it covered. You guys have fun." Eero would owe him—big time—for this, Blaze decided.

"Really?" Aura looked up at him with wide, brown eyes, and that too-big smile. Blaze wondered if she realized that she looked like one of those smoosh faced dogs when she got excited like that. He could practically hear her tail wagging.

"Yeah, I could use a break myself," he lied.

"Great! Just monitor him, he bruises easy and is a total lightweight," Aura cautioned, the too-big smile slipping a little in her concern for her friend.

"I'm not an invalid, Aura!" Fable shouted over the music.

"I know, sweetie!"

Blaze rolled his eyes, turning to head for the booth without a word. Fable followed behind and flopped down once they reached the seats. "You don't have to sit with me. I'm fine."

Blaze snorted. "Like I was going to stay by myself with those two horn-dogs." Fable blinked at him in question, and Blaze hooked a thumb over his shoulder towards where they'd left their friends.

"Wha—ooooooh," Fable exhaled when his eyes fell upon Eero and Aura who had begun grinding together on the dance floor. "Why didn't they just come by themselves?"

"You can't just come to a club with two people." Blaze shrugged.

"You can't?" Fable's eyes had fixed on Blaze; he cocked his head in confusion. "Why can't you?"

"I don't know, that's just what Eero said. Look, sit tight, I'll grab us some waters," Blaze muttered. His eyes flicked over to the bar to see how packed it was. *Not too bad, thankfully.*

"Oh, yeah, sure." Fable nodded.

Blaze turned on his heel to weave through dancing couples, and drunk groups of girls, before he made it to the bar. Once he had their waters and was headed back, he was surprised to find Fable still sitting exactly where he'd left him. "Are you always this obedient?"

Fable looked back from where he'd been staring across the dance floor, and shrugged. "Aura was right, I'm getting close to my limit. I don't want to get sloppy drunk." He grabbed one of the waters and took a careful sip.

"Right," Blaze agreed incredulously. "So, this is you getting wild, huh? No knitting needles?"

Fable laughed softly, shaking his head. "I don't get wild, 'least not anymore."

"Why not?"

Mismatched eyes clouded over with a memory as Fable seemed to stare at something that Blaze couldn't see. Then he shook himself and shrugged. "I used to in college."

Blaze waited for him to say more, but he didn't. Amber eyes drank in the other man as Fable sipped his water with his eyes focused on the dancers once more. "You and Aura went to the same college?"

"We went to the same veterinarian school," Fable confirmed. "We've been friends ever since."

"Why didn't you move to the city with her to begin

with?" *I'm just making conversation,* Blaze told himself. *I'm not really interested.* Except, he kind of was. Fable was a mystery wrapped in an enigma, stuffed into the body of a person, and Blaze wanted to solve it.

"Oh, I went home for a few years. There was a clinic there, and my mom was worried sick about me, so I thought I'd just set up shop back home. I mean, everyone had grown up, right? It wouldn't be the same as it was," Fable had gone off on a tangent, the words flowing in a steady stream. Blaze wasn't sure what he was talking about, but there seemed to be no stopping him at this point. *Shit, is he really that drunk?* He hadn't sounded like it a minute ago. "Surely, everyone could get off their bullshit, right?"

"Uh, right," Blaze answered, brows creased. "So, what happened?"

"Nothing had changed! Small town, small minds," Fable huffed. Blaze wasn't sure he was following, but he nodded anyway. Fable definitely was that drunk. "It was all, well, how can you like guys? You had a girlfriend in college? What are you gay now?"

Something clicked, or he thought it did anyway, and Blaze nodded. "People are dumbasses."

"*Such* dumbasses," Fable agreed, pointing at him as if he held the secret to life.

"Hey! We aren't talking about those assholes again, are we? I told you to stop that," Aura heaved a sigh, flopping down into Fable's lap. Her arms looped around his neck, and she pressed a kiss to his cheek, leaving behind a glossy lip-print.

"Which assholes are we not talking about?" Eero asked, forcing Blaze deeper into the booth with his hip.

"Fable is bi." Aura shrugged.

"Wow, Aura, just dive right into it and out me," Fable

groaned, shoving her off his lap into the booth next to him. She struggled for a moment but ultimately sat up, glaring daggers at him.

"What? That's what you were getting at. Just much slower," she countered, a little smirk splitting her lips. The expression was arguably worse than the too-big smile. "Right? You were trying to tell Blaze how the idiots back home couldn't grasp the concept?"

"Jeezus, am I ever *not* going to be coming out?" Fable cried, dropping his head down to the table with a thunk that made Blaze wince.

"I know, darling." Aura pet his hair like she might a cat. "It's ridiculous. Anyway, Fable was trying to say—in his roundabout-Fable-way—that it was hard living in a town where the only options were gay or straight."

"Plus, no one would date me there," Fable added, his voice muffled by the sticky surface of the table.

"Right, plus, no one would date him there."

"Why not?" Eero asked, his face dusted pink from drinking and dancing, scrunched up in confusion.

Blaze groaned, scrubbing at the back of his neck—they were all drunk. He would have to make sure both of the stupid humans got home safely. Not only that, he was learning much more about Fable than he ever wanted to. He could feel Eero beside him, soaking it all up like a sponge. Fan-fracking-tastic. He'd never hear the end of this, whatever *this* was.

Fable mumbled something unintelligible into the table, and Aura took it upon herself to translate. "Everyone thought he'd cheat on them."

Eero snorted loudly. "What? This fluffy teddy bear? A cheater?"

"That's what I said!" Aura giggled; her hand stopped petting Fable's hair.

"I'm not a teddy bear!" Fable growled, lifting his head from the table to glare at both of them. Blaze snorted under his breath. For all his trying, Fable looked about as threatening as a hamster.

"What are you then?" Aura countered, her lips twitching with that smirk again.

Blaze rubbed his temples as the pair descended into something very similar to sibling bickering. He got up to get another round of waters, and when he returned, he found that they were still going at it.

"Wait, so you two dated in college?" Eero asked, cutting through the senseless chatter.

"Yeah, for like a week." Aura shrugged.

"And?" There was Eero, always needling. He had to know everything about everyone. Annoying—is what it was. "What happened?"

"It was weird and gross," Fable answer.

"Hey!" Aura shoved him, and Fable nearly stumbled out of the booth.

"I never said *you* were weird and gross," Fable argued, rubbing at his shoulder. "No need to bruise me, damn it."

"Sorry," Aura muttered, sobering a little. Then she turned back to Eero. "What he meant to say, was that we're too much like family. So, what about you two? Did you ever date?" The solemn expression from a moment ago was replaced again with her wicked smirk.

"Who? Each other?" Eero countered before descending into a round of snickers that made Blaze scowl.

"Weird and gross, right?" Fable bit back a laugh, his mismatched eyes crinkling at the edges.

"*So* weird and gross," Eero confirmed, and then they were all laughing.

Blaze's brows creased in annoyance. He didn't enjoy being laughed at, never had, and as his hands tightened into fists in his lap, he could feel them heating. He bit back a snarl before it could rip from his lips. "Right then. If you assholes are done insulting me, I'm heading home," he groused. "You two got a car picking you up?"

"We'll just grab a cab," Fable shrugged.

"I've got someone coming to get us, don't worry about us, Mister White Knight." Aura gave him a salute.

Blaze blinked at her, frowning deeply. It was almost enough to make him miss Fable flopping his head back down onto the sticky table, *almost*. "Right, he gonna be okay?" Blaze asked, his amber eyes fixed on the tuft of messy hair, and the slight flush on the tips of Fable's ears.

"Yeah, he'll be fine, I'll stay with him tonight. We don't let Fable-wable stay alone after he's been drinking, do we?" Aura reached down to pinch Fable's check between her fingers.

"Stop it." Fable glared at her, swatting her hand away.

"Great. Let's head out then," Blaze announced, and looked down at Eero with a quirked brow. The dryad nodded, and they both stood. Aura pulled out her phone to text someone, and then the four made their way through the club into the sticky summer air. "We'll wait with you till your car gets here." Blaze carefully avoided the questioning look from Eero.

"You really don't have to, it might be a bit," Aura argued.

"We've got time," Eero assured.

The four stood leaning against the wall of a closed café, waiting. Fable, Aura, and Eero chatted like they were old friends, which was nice. It meant Blaze only had to grunt in response sometimes to make it seem like he was involved in the conversation. After a night out, he appreciated not having to be any more social than necessary. He thought they would talk themselves out, but they didn't stop until a little red economy car pulled up.

The driver wound down the window, and a redhead grinned over at them. "Well, hello, darlings," they purred. "Need a lift?"

"Is that?" Eero asked under his breath to Blaze.

"Yup," Blaze confirmed, frowning when Gwydion met his eyes.

"Thanks for staying with us! You two are real gentlemen, aren't they, Gwydion?" Aura asked Gwydion—who had climbed out to open the back door for Fable to flop into the back seat.

"Oh, definitely." Gwydion's golden eyes lit up with mirth. Blaze glared at them, wondering if he could bore a hole into the center of their forehead with just his eyes.

It didn't work. And soon enough both humans were loaded up into the back of the car. Fable and Aura waved goodbye before Gwydion sped off, and Blaze exhaled, his shoulders sagging.

"What do you think they're up to?" Eero asked.

"Don't know. Don't care. Can't be good, though," Blaze muttered. "I've got a dog to get home to. I'll see you later." Without waiting for Eero to answer, he started down the street.

SEVEN

Fable was fairly sure—no, he was positive—he had made an ass of himself at the bar. Not only that, but the drinking seemed to have shaken something loose in his subconscious. What he was once certain was nothing more than vivid dreams suddenly felt like so much more. Like a glimpse into a life he had never lived. The longer they haunted him, the more a feeling of knowing them to be true sank into his bones.

Still, he did his best to ignore them and buried himself further in his work. He didn't have time to be distracted by dreams, or memories, or hallucinations, or whatever they were. Not when there were patients to see. Summer was their busiest time of year, as so many pets were more active during those months. That meant more of them were getting injured or sick from eating something they shouldn't outside. So, he could bury his head in the sand, at least for a couple of months.

When it was finally cold enough to pull out the old knit sweater with the elbow patches, things had calmed down, and it seemed he could no longer ignore the dreams. With his days less strenuous and full, he wasn't as tired when he got home as he'd been. Making sleep more elusive.

3:23AM

The glaring red light from his cable box screamed at him as Fable clutched his chest. He inhaled deeply, squeezing his eyes shut to regain control over the fight-or-flight instinct that accompanied one of the vivid dreams, which were now a regular occurrence.

"It's so weird," he whispered to himself, remembering that boy. The one with the pale hair and strikingly cruel amber eyes. "He looked like Blaze." Fable shook himself, laughing at the insanity of the idea. "No."

Sweat trickled down the side of his neck, and he flopped back into bed, kicking the thick plaid comforter away, which earned him a grumble from the little mutt at the foot of the bed.

"Sorry," he muttered, rolling onto his side to cool the skin on his back. Fable squeezed his eyes shut and tried to will himself back to sleep. He counted to ten. When that didn't work, he counted to fifty. He opened his eyes again to glare at the clock.

3:25AM

Two minutes! It had only been two minutes! With a groan, he grabbed his phone to scroll through social media, hoping the mind-numbing effort of seeing other people's pictures would calm him. Twenty or so little hearts later, he rechecked the clock.

3:34AM

"Oh, for Petey's sake!" He threw the spare pillow at the cable box. It missed, thankfully, and dropped to the floor with a soft thud. He needed something to take his mind off of the image of that boy, the one with the eyes so much like Blaze's, and a body full of scars. It was too early to go for a run, and surely no one would be awake right then.

Well, maybe not no one.

Before he could second guess the notion, he sent a text to Gwydion's number.

> Fable 3:36AM
>> Hi
>> It's Fable
>> Are you up?

Fable wasn't expecting a response, despite what Gwydion had said. Surely no one, not even a smutty romance novelist, was up at 3:30 in the morning. He dropped his phone to his chest to stare listlessly up at the ceiling. When it buzzed, he lifted it to glare at the too-bright screen, expecting a text, and instead, he found the decline and answer buttons glaring back at him.

"Hello?" he asked when he answered it.

"What's up, sugar? Can't sleep?" Gwydion's voice rolled cheerfully through the speaker. They sounded wide awake and in a good mood. How was that even possible?

"You could have just texted," Fable replied lamely in a groggy voice.

"I don't do the text thing usually. It's too impersonal. Besides, I enjoy hearing people's voices when they call to ask me for a favor." There was a tapping noise in the background that Fable could only assume was Gwydion working on a manuscript or something.

"I'm not—I don't need—it's not about a favor," Fable huffed.

The tapping stopped for a moment, and Gwydion laughed softly—a light, whimsical sound. "Of course not, darling. I know that."

"Uh—right." This was moronic, Fable decided. "Look, I'm sorry to bother you. I'll just—I'll just let you get back to work."

Gwydion let out a soft sigh, and Fable could almost imagine them leaning back in their chair to get comfortable. "Fable, you aren't bothering me. I gave you my number in case you needed someone to talk to, and you do." Without the darlings, and sweeties, and aunties, Gwydion sounded much older than they ever had before. Fable wondered how old they were, they looked so young. "So, talk."

Fable nodded, exhaling deeply as he rolled onto his side again, pressing the phone into the pillow with his ear. "What did you mean when you said that dreams were us trying to remember our past lives?"

"I thought I was clear about that, sweetheart." Gwydion chuckled softly. Suddenly they were back to the flouncy, nonchalant tone of voice. As if nothing mattered, and life was a game. Fable wished he could be that way. "There are some who believe that dreams are buried memories from past lives we are trying to reconcile with our current existence."

"So, fighting a dragon," Fable mumbled softly.

"Yes, fighting a dragon."

"But dragons aren't real," Fable argued, feeling silly. Of course dragons weren't real, so why was he even considering that the dream was a memory?

"Hmm..." Gwydion hummed softly as the tapping resumed. "That scientists know of."

"What?"

They laughed, a soft rustling sound showing that they

were shaking their head. "Maybe they were, we don't know. We weren't around in the medieval times, were we? Regardless, the dragon could be a metaphor."

"It didn't feel like a metaphor, it felt like a dragon," Fable grumbled petulantly.

"Tell me everything from your dream," Gwydion insisted.

"This is silly."

"No, it's not. Just do it."

So, Fable did. He relayed all the bits and pieces. The angry man and the carriage. The feeling of drowning. The shining scales of the dragon. Through all of it, Gwydion listened, letting him talk himself out. By the time he finished, his voice no longer sounded groggy, and he felt more rested than he had in months.

"And they feel so real," Fable insisted, scrubbing at his sleep-crusted eyes. "And that man, he looked so much like Blaze."

Gwydion was silent for so long Fable almost wondered if they had fallen asleep. "Think about it this way. Maybe it wasn't a dragon. Maybe it was just an enormous jerk who needed bringing down a peg."

"Umm... okay?"

"And maybe it was Blaze. Maybe you two idiots have been dancing around each other for centuries."

"That sounds nuts," Fable snorted.

"Life *is* nuts, darling. It never makes any kind of good sense, and why should this either?" Gwydion asked. The question sounded rhetorical, but Gwydion waited for an answer.

"I guess it shouldn't," Fable stuttered, cheeks aflame. He felt rather like a child being scolded by their teacher when they didn't understand a simple math problem. Two plus two is four, not five.

Gwydion tutted to themselves in thought, then seeming to decide about something they said, "Why don't we meet for breakfast in an hour? This will all make a lot more sense if we talk in person."

"Um... okay?" Fable said—again—feeling like a complete idiot.

"Fabulous! I'll meet you at Thelma's," Gwydion giggled into the phone and then they hung up.

Fable sat for a moment, looking at his phone in confusion before he pulled himself out of bed to glare at the clock again.

4:39AM

He rolled out of bed, tugged on a pair of day-old jeans from the floor, and a loose-fitting knit sweater before brushing his teeth. After trying to run a comb through his disastrously matted hair for five straight minutes, he gave up and headed out to meet Gwydion.

The redhead was waiting for Fable when he arrived; they had two cups of coffee in front of them, and a little grin on their features. For all the world it looked like Gwydion had spent four hours getting ready, not the less than one Fable assumed they had. Their long red hair was set into neat ringlets over one shoulder, golden eyes lined perfectly, and they were wearing an off the shoulder green sweater. Fable flopped unceremoniously into the booth across from them. "How can you look so chipper right now?"

"Good coffee." Gwydion giggled, scooting the other mug towards Fable's freckled fingers. He took it, prepping it with creamer before taking a slow sip and letting it wake him from the inside out. All the while, Gwydion waited patiently. Once Fable was more coherent, they smiled knowingly at him. "Now, as I was saying, what if all of that did happen?"

"But it didn't," Fable insisted, rubbing at the bridge of his nose under the thick-framed, black glasses.

"By land and by sky," Gwydion murmured to themselves.

"Huh?"

With one red brow quirked, Gwydion reached out and pressed the tip of their finger to the back of Fable's hand. Glitter—or dust motes maybe—twirled around the point where skin touched skin, and a shock ran through Fable, causing him to jerk his hand away. Fable opened his mouth to ask what the hell that had been, but then his two-toned eyes widened as all the memories came flooding back. The village near the sea. The small family he'd raised in London. The war and the carnage that came with it. All tied together by a pair of angry amber eyes. When Fable's eyes focused once more, he scowled. "He killed me."

"Yeah, a couple of times," Gwydion chuckled in wry amusement with a little shrug that slid the sweater down further to reveal a creamy shoulder. "But—here you are, again."

"And you, what? Brought me back over, and over, so I would have to deal with him and his shit again?" Fury bubbled up hot and fresh in Fable's throat, threatening to choke him. How dare Blaze show up here, now, just when Fable had gotten his life together again! How dare Gwydion bring him back over, and over to suffer the same fate!

Gwydion set down their coffee, letting out a soft, tired sigh. "I only did what you asked me to do. You wanted to tame the dragon, I gave you that ability."

"But you didn't give me the power to do it, did you?" Fable accused. He felt irrationally angry. Gwydion was right, he had asked for this. He just hadn't really known what he was asking for.

"No, I just provided you with the time you'd need. As I told you the first time we met, there is no magic spell to tame a dragon."

"Then how do you tame a dragon?" Fable shouted, drawing the attention of some of the other early morning patrons. He didn't care. None of it mattered. If he screwed up this chance, he'd just be reborn and start over.

With another careful sip of their coffee, Gwydion frowned. "As with any animal and most people, there is only trust."

"That is ridiculous! He killed me!" Fable whispered harshly so as not to be overheard, his eyes flashing danger-ously. "I'm supposed to get *him* to trust *me*? I don't trust him!"

"No, I suppose you don't. But that is between the two of you, just as it was before. Now, I'm sorry, but I must get back to work. I have a deadline to meet." Gwydion's expres-sion had turned sad, as if the witch had hoped for better this time. As if they'd thought perhaps this would be the time Fable would understand. They slid a few bills onto the table and murmured, "for the coffee," before disappearing out into the city again.

Fable sat at the table for a long while, seething and sipping his now-cold coffee. People drifted in and out, but the waitress avoided his booth, not even bothering to stop and refill his mug. When he finally looked at his phone to check the time, it was 8:00AM, and he'd decided.

If dragon taming is what he was destined to do, then dragon taming is what he would do!

With a nod, he paid for his coffee and headed back to his apartment to get ready for work.

FABLE'S LEG bounced where it was curled up underneath him in his desk chair. He didn't know why he was so nervous—no, wait; he knew exactly why he was so nervous. Setting up a meeting with one's eternal nemesis to, quote-unquote, talk things out, was a nerve-wracking experience. Not to mention he was still coming to terms with what he now knew of himself, and his history with the dragon. It was... a lot.

"Got a hot date?" Aura asked, poking her head around the doorframe to grin at him. "Is it Blaze? Please say it's Blaze."

"What?" Fable looked up from where he'd been staring blankly at his phone waiting for Blaze's response.

Aura bounced on her toes a little as she trotted to his desk, her bob of neat brunette hair bouncing along with her. "You guys seemed to get along great when we went out a while back. And Eero and I hoped that you'd—" She shrugged, dropping into the chair on the other side of his desk. "It'd be nice to go on double dates."

Fable's jaw dropped, his eyes meeting Aura's in utter shock. Surely, she didn't think — "That's ridiculous!" he squeaked.

"Is it?" Aura's words were incredulous, and there was a knowing glimmer in her eyes.

"I don't even like him! He's-He's-He's—" Fable scrambled for words. He couldn't tell her all that he knew about Blaze, but any other words seemed to stall on his tongue.

"Hot?" she suggested with a giggle. "Charming? Roguish? Like something out of a romance novel?"

"He's an asshole," Fable finished flatly, narrowing his eyes at her. "I don't date assholes."

Brown eyes blinked back at him as she pondered his words. "I mean, he's not the nicest guy, but I wouldn't call him an asshole. From what I've heard from Eero he seems to have a soft spot buried under all those rough layers."

"Like an onion?" Fable smirked, biting back a laugh.

"No, like a parfait," Aura giggled, shaking her head. Fable laughed too. Some of the tension eased from his gut at the laughter, and he let himself ponder what Aura had said. Blaze did have a soft spot for his dog. It wasn't much, but it was a start—wasn't it? Maybe he had changed a little over the centuries. "Either way, give him a shot. I think he likes you." With that, she hopped up and trotted out.

Fable's phone buzzed on the desk. He looked down to read Blaze's response, and the tension coiled in his gut again.

Blaze 4:13PM
> Coffee sounds good
> See you at 6

"Well, there you go, Fable. No way out of it now," Fable breathed to himself.

FABLE ARRIVED a half hour early so he could find them a seat in the secluded corner of the little coffee shop. He hoped that with them tucked away, people wouldn't overhear their conversation. He didn't particularly want to be carted off to an institution. Slipping out of his jacket, he hung it over the back of the chair, then went to order himself a cup of hot chocolate.

Fingers drummed nervously on his thigh as he waited

for his order, tuning out the rest of the shop to keep his breathing steady. Maybe he should have gone for a run first? It would have worn down some of his nervous energy. But then he would have had to shower, and that would have just made him more nervous. No, this was better. He didn't want to be rushed.

"You're early," a voice grumbled near his ear.

"Blaze!" Fable jumped, nearly knocking someone's coffee from their hand. He muttered a soft apology to them and turned to the taller man. "I uh—I didn't expect you for another," he looked down at his phone, wrinkling his nose a little. "Five minutes?"

Blaze shrugged, a teasing smile tugging at the corner of his lips. "Guess I'm early too."

"You, um—" Fable swallowed roughly, the nerves fluttering up into his throat. He'd been so angry—irate, even—that he'd planned this meeting without properly considering what would happen once they were face to face. "Do you want a coffee?"

"Nah, I don't drink coffee."

"Then, why did you—?" Fable frowned at the thought.

"You said you wanted to talk," Blaze answered. "Come on, let's sit."

"Oh, right, we're just over here," Fable gestured to the chairs he'd saved for them in the back corner. He swallowed around the feeling of bile rising in his throat. What was he going to say? How was he going to explain this? Would Blaze think he was crazy? Gwydion hadn't told him how they kept meeting. They didn't say if Blaze were reincarnated too, or if he'd just lived that long. What if Blaze didn't remember it?

Blaze flopped into the seat across from him, legs spread wide as he got comfortable. "So, what d'you want?"

With a deep breath, Fable met those all too familiar amber eyes. The scar that ran from the man's temple to jaw caught Fable's eye. There was no mistaking it now, there had been no reincarnation, this was the exact same person. The dragon. "I remember. Everything."

Something flashed behind Blaze's eyes—fear, maybe? Apprehension? Then it disappeared, and Blaze wrinkled his brows. "You mean from the bar? Damn, I didn't think you were that ou—"

"No, not from the bar," Fable cut him off to clarify. He wouldn't let Blaze sidestep this. They needed to get it over with. If they were going to live in the same city, they needed this out in the open so that Fable could live his life in peace. "I remember the village."

Blaze's eyes flicked over Fable's face, and then he looked away quickly. "So what?" he scoffed with a shrug. His lips pressed into a thin line, and he refused to meet Fable's eyes again.

"So what?" Fable sputtered. "What do you mean, '*so what?*'"

"I mean, *so what* do you want from me? An apology? Because you ain't getting one," Blaze snarled, his eyes flashing dangerously.

Had he been expecting an apology? Not really. But Fable had been expecting some indication that Blaze had grown as a person. That they could put this behind them. That Blaze, at the very least, felt sorry that he'd hurt Fable so many times. "No, but I wanted to talk about it."

"There isn't anything to talk about, dipshit."

"There is! You-I-we—we are connected," Fable stuttered.

"Connected?" Blaze asked, disgust dripping from the word.

"Yes, connected," Fable insisted. He could feel slow anger rising in his blood, but he did his best to swallow it down. "We've been dancing around each other for—"

"We aren't connected," Blaze cut him off with a contemptuous snort. "You're just some stupid ass kid who didn't know how to keep his nose out of other people's business. You didn't know when to shut your damn mouth then, and you don't know when to now. Maybe if you had, you *wouldn't* have died all those times."

Fable's mouth opened and closed as he tried to get his brain to think of words to say. Something. Anything that would bite back at Blaze the way he'd just cut Fable down. "Well, you're a–you're a–you're a—"

"A what? Can't get any words past that tiny brain of yours, dumbass?" Blaze jeered, leaning in towards Fable.

Fable could smell sulfur, and he wondered if the dragon always smelled that way or if he were about to light Fable on fire. Wouldn't that make quite the sight? "You're a bully!" Fable spat, finally.

"Yeah?" Blaze asked, pressing closer, the smell of fire growing stronger.

"Yeah!" Fable countered, leaning forward as well. Two people could play that game.

Blaze let out a short, sharp laugh that made Fable's stomach lurch. "Well, I'd rather be a bully than an idiot. Tame a dragon? You? Please," he scoffed.

"Jerk!" Fable shoved Blaze hard by his shoulders.

"You moronic, weak, spineless, worthless, pathetic human," Blaze countered, spitting the last word like it was a curse. Then he shoved back, harder. Fable heard more than felt his chair stumble backward. He righted himself before it fell all the way and took him with it, but only just so.

His hands shook—a head injury is exactly how their first

fight had ended. "Well, fork you too, you mean giraffe!" Fable shouted, standing up abruptly. Blaze's eyes had widened as he watched the other man stand, a strange expression twisted his lips. Fable wasn't sure if it was disgust, or shock, or confusion, or some mixture of the three. He didn't care. He'd had enough. "Find another vet," Fable seethed lowly.

"What?" Blaze's voice was barely above a whisper now, as those amber eyes widened further.

"You heard me," Fable panted in his fury. "Find another God damn vet. I'm done. We're done. We've been toxic to one another for centuries, and I'm tired of being your punching bag. Enough is enough. I give. You can't be tamed, or trained, or reasoned with, or even befriended and I'm not wasting what time I have on someone who can't get their head out of their ass long enough to see when someone wants to help them. Next time you have a problem with your dog, call someone else." With that, Fable headed for the door.

"Oi! You can't just—" Blaze tried to argue, standing to follow him.

"Oh, I *can* just. I've cut people out of my life before because they weren't any good for me, and I'll be damned if I let whatever *this* is, hurt me anymore. See you in our next life, Blaze." He stormed out into the city street, not looking back. With shaking hands, he pulled his phone from his pocket and dialed Gwydion.

"Ah, Fable, darling. I was hoping—"

"I quit," Fable cut them off.

"You what?" Gwydion asked, and Fable could almost imagine them blinking wide golden eyes at him.

"Find yourself another dragon tamer, and leave me out of this shit from now on. Whatever I asked for, take it back.

I don't want it anymore," his words left him in a rush. Then he hung up and started the long trudge home. Maybe he should have hailed a cab, or called for a car, but right then, all he wanted was to stomp through the city streets until he had control of his breathing.

EIGHT

"What did you do?" the tinny voice on the other side of the phone growled into Blaze's ear.

"What the hell do you want, witch?" Blaze snarled back. This would teach him to pick up phone calls from numbers he didn't recognize. It was never anything good. It was always a telemarketer, or someone trying to scam him out of money, or a witch who had never learned to mind their own damn business.

"Fable just called me," Gwydion said, anger still making their voice ragged around the edges. Gone was the smooth, confident tone that made the world seem like a plaything. In its place was the fury of a god—or a vague facsimile of one, anyway. "He told me to take it back! He's says he's quitting, and I should take the magic back!"

Blaze snorted. Of course, Fable had been in touch with Gwydion as soon as he'd left the coffee shop. Fable had had enough of Blaze's shit, that much was clear. So why wouldn't he react by telling Gwydion to call the whole thing off? "That's his business, not mine," Blaze muttered indifferently.

"What did you do?" Gwydion demanded again.

The image of Fable stumbling back in his chair, nearly smacking his head against the hard tile floor, flashed through Blaze's mind again. His stomach rolled, and he had to breathe deeply through his nose to keep from vomiting. It was so eerily similar to that first time. How could he have made that mistake again? "I didn't do anything to that little idiot. Leave me alone."

"You stupid shit," Gwydion seethed.

"You know what, I don't have to take this shit from you," Blaze seethed with finality, then promptly hung up. Running a shaking hand over his face, he took a breath to calm himself. When the phone rang again with the same number, he hit ignore and blocked the number. Was it childish? Yes. Could Gwydion get around it easily? Also, yes. But that didn't stop him.

INSTEAD OF GOING HOME to change, he headed straight for the station. Anger and the image of Fable's head split open simmered in the back of his mind, waiting to take over if he let it. So, he loaded himself onto the treadmill and started running. He ran until his breathing grew ragged. He ran until the image in the mirror of himself blurred with sweat. While he had pushed the memory away, the anger continued. Who did that runt think he was? Here they were, hundreds of years later, and that idiot mage still hadn't learned any self-preservation skills. If he'd been smart—which he obviously was not —he would have avoided Blaze like the plague. He'd pretend he knew nothing, and they could both get on with their lives. But no, Fable had gotten up the balls to confront the dragon. Seriously? Where did that kid get off?

"Dude, are you okay?" A voice filtered into his thoughts. Eero. Blaze ignored him and kept running. He had put headphones in for a reason for frack sake. He didn't want to hear anyone! He wanted to be alone with his rage! Eero, as per usual, didn't take the hint. The redhead moved to stand in front of the treadmill, arms crossed over his muscled chest.

Blaze ripped a headphone from his ear to bark at Eero. "What do you want, shit for brains?"

Eero scowled but gave no indication that he was insulted. He probably wasn't, the guy was that dense. "Are you feeling all right?"

A snarl turned up the dragon's top lip as Blaze opened his mouth to tell Eero that he was fine, and to piss off. Then he could enjoy running himself ragged in peace and do his best to forget all the shit that had hit the fan in the last few hours. Amber eyes flicked up to drink in his reflection. Blaze's lightly tanned skin was pink, flushed all over with exertion, but his sweat was evaporating much too quickly. He took a moment to focus and felt the heat in his palms. Yeah, if he so much as touched the handle of this stupid ass machine, it'd be nothing more than ash beneath his feet. Shit.

"No," he answered honestly.

With a sigh, Eero's shoulders sagged. "Let's talk," he offered softly, moving to turn off the machine for his friend. Then he headed for the locker room without a second glance back at Blaze.

It took a moment before Blaze was in control of his anger enough to lift the hem of his shirt, and wipe the sweat from his face. He followed Eero to the locker room, not expecting Eero to be waiting for him with his own anger etched into his angular face. The dryad took a step forward, backing Blaze into a corner, a brow quirked expectantly. Instead of asking, Eero stayed silent and waited—that's how he always did it, he waited. Eero would remain quiet for hours, waiting Blaze out until he finally came clean. That's probably why they were friends, Eero wouldn't take any of Blaze's shit, but he almost never got confrontational about it.

"What?" Blaze asked—he wasn't in the mood for spilling his guts today. He wanted to work his shift and go home to his damn dog.

"Dude, you're such an asshole." Eero shook his head as though he were disappointed in Blaze.

Blaze thought better of asking what the hell he was talking about, he knew. Aura must have talked, stupid, gossipy, busy body. "I'm the asshole?" he half-shouted as fury set his blood on fire again. "I'm the asshole? That little shit comes at me, demanding I apologize to him, and for what? For all the shit that was centuries ago? And I'm the asshole? No, he's the asshole! Couldn't he just let sleeping dogs lie? Couldn't we just have ignored it, and moved on with our lives? We didn't have to talk about all of that. We could have just moved on. But no!"

Eero eyed him blandly. "Maybe you *should* apologize to him. You did kill him, after all. Twice, if my count is correct."

"Those were accidents! Every time was an accident!"

"More reason to apologize. Put all of this—"

"I'm not apologizing!" Blaze roared; smoke billowed threateningly from his throat. "You can forget it!"

"Then you may want to find another vet. Cause neither he nor Aura are going to put up with your shit," Eero said simply.

"He'll get over it," Blaze muttered as he deflated. He was sure Fable would get over it, and then they could just go back to—whatever the hell they had been doing. Right?

"Yeah, sure he will, man. Keep telling yourself that." Eero rolled his eyes and left Blaze there in the locker room without another word.

AS IT WOULD HAPPEN, Fable didn't get over it—or, at least, he didn't look like he was going to anytime soon. The first few texts Blaze sent were left on 'read'—unanswered. After that, it didn't even look like they were being seen. When Blaze tried to call on his way home, the line rolled right over to voicemail. "I think that little shit blocked my number," he muttered with a scowl.

He was too tired to be furious; he decided. It would take too much work to get himself worked up into a rage. Plus, he'd likely lose his phone in the process, so what was the point? Instead, he leaned back against the hard-plastic seat and closed his eyes. Half dozing, he listened to the announcements for the stops through the garbled speakers of the train.

They were a stop from his apartment when the train slammed to a halt. A man with a very large, very full cup of coffee in front of Blaze stumbled forward. His coffee slipped from his fingers, spilling all over Blaze's jeans as it toppled to the floor. "Are you serious right now with this shit!" Blaze shouted, standing to his feet abruptly. His jeans dripped onto the hard floor of the train, creating a puddle.

"Oh, my heavens, I'm so sorry," the man gasped, jerking away from the furious fireman.

"You're sorry?" Blaze asked. He felt his hands burn at

his sides. The phone—still clutched in his hand—disintegrated into nothing but smoke and ash. "Shit!" he hissed, letting the remnants fall into the puddle of coffee at his feet.

"We apologize for the inconvenience, passengers," someone said over the loudspeaker—it must be the driver of this shitty little train. "We're experiencing some technical difficulties and hope to be up and moving again soon. Until then, please be patient with us, we'll have this sorted out as soon as possible."

Soon meant two hours later.

By the time Blaze made it back to his apartment, the coffee on his pants had dried, leaving behind a sticky mess, and he was sweating from the sweltering temperatures of the train—making him even stickier. His stomach gave a disgruntled growl. *Right, add hungry to the list*, he thought bitterly. To top it all off, when he opened the door to his apartment, he found a mess. Bakugo, in his boredom, had demolished every toy he could get his teeth on, dragged a roll of toilet paper across the floor, pissed on the leg of the couch, and had found something disgusting to roll in. Blaze didn't even want to think about what it was, but assumed it was something from the trash.

"Are you shitting me right now?" Blaze roared. The little dog whimpered, tucking himself under the futon to hide from his owner. "Oh, no you don't, you little shit. We're going outside."

It took a full ten minutes to get the mutt from under the futon and leashed before Blaze was dragging him down the hall. Just as they were about to load onto the elevator, a door opened. "Is that a dog?" a woman asked, her eyes narrowing on the mutt.

"What does it look like to you? A dolphin?" Blaze snarked. He had exactly zero patience left for some wannabe yuppy in knock-off Calvin Klein sneakers. Zero! "Of course, it's a dog you dipshit!"

"This building has a no pets policy." She crossed her arms over her chest, her nose curling in disgust as Bakugo turned to yip at her, his tail wagging merrily.

"So what? You gonna tell on me? Are we five? Piss off, bitch," he growled, scooping up Bakugo and climbing into the elevator. He had just enough time to flip her the bird before the door slid shut.

His building super was waiting for Blaze when he got back upstairs. The pompous old man leaned against Blaze's door; eyes stern. "You're out," he said once Blaze was close enough.

"What're you talking about?" Blaze scowled. He clutched the little dog tighter into his side, reminding himself to stay calm. "I'm out?"

"Either you get rid of the mutt, or you move out. You've got forty-eight hours." He said nothing else, just turned on his heel and walked away.

"You know what, fine! I was moving out anyway! Pompous old windbag!" Blaze shouted after him, seething. The man didn't turn back or say anything more, he just left. The door slammed behind Blaze, and he smacked his head back against it with a groan. He inhaled a shaking breath, scrubbing at his face. "This is going to suck, Baku," he mumbled to the little dog.

Bakugo's only response was to yip happily and wag his nubby tail.

"You're right, I better get it over with." He set the dog on the ground, took a deep breath, and shouted. "Gwydion!"

It wasn't the first time he'd called on the witch, but it would be the first time he had asked them for help. His gut twisted when they didn't automatically appear as they had before.

"Come on, Gwydion, I need a favor," he pleaded, staring at the ceiling. He was not above begging for the witch to remove whatever hex they'd put on him.

"What do *you* want?" Gwydion barked into his ear, causing Blaze to jump. "First, you want me to mind my own business, and now you need a favor? And what happened to your apartment? This place is a sty! Do you always live like this?"

"Whatever you did because you were mad at me," Blaze started, swallowing thickly. "I need you to take it off. I can't deal with bad luck like this. It's gonna kill me."

Gwydion snorted. "Dragons can't be killed."

"Does that matter right now? I'm asking you to—"

"Besides, this isn't the result of a jinx. This is Karma biting you in the ass for being a bitch to Fable." Gwydion shrugged. They picked their way carefully across the mess of the floor, avoiding getting their nude pumps dirty. "You're just getting exactly what you deserve, finally."

"Fine, it's karma, whatever! Fix it?" He'd fall to his knees and beg if he had to. Blaze couldn't have another day like this one, not if he wanted to keep his record of never reducing a living creature to ash.

"I can't." They settled delicately onto the corner of the sofa; posture perfect but somehow relaxed. "That's Karma's deal. She's a bitch of a whole different color, and I don't fool with her magic. The only thing you can do is make up with Fable."

"Fine then. I need a place for Baku and I to stay until I can find a new apartment. Just for a few weeks."

Gwydion's golden eyes narrowed on him in thought, their full red lips tugging down at the corners. It was clear they weren't happy with him, and why should they be? Blaze had done nothing but insult, berate, and shout at Gwydion. The witch had no reason at all to help him. After a moment, they nodded. "Okay, but my house, my rules."

Blaze nodded quickly. "I'll go pack a bag."

"What about your—" They took a sweeping look around, nose turning up in disgust at the décor. "All of this."

"The place is furnished, none of it's mine." Blaze shrugged and headed to his room to pack up his and Bakugo's things.

"Hmm..." Gwydion hummed thoughtfully.

AN HOUR later found Blaze dropping his large duffle onto the lightly varnished hardwood floors of Gwydion's apartment. Bakugo sat beside him, looking around at the wide-open space much as his owner was—in awe.

"Tea, darling?" Gwydion called, trotting to the kitchen.

"Uh, yeah, sure," Blaze mumbled, scrubbing at the back of his neck.

Gwydion came back a moment later with a dainty tea tray that they set on the sleek, modern coffee table. "Why didn't you ask your dryad friend?"

"Eero?" Blaze's confusion knit his brows. "He lives with like five other guys in a tiny-ass apartment. There wouldn't have been any room for me there." With a huff, he dropped onto the tufted sofa next to Gwydion, and took his tea gratefully.

"And your other friends?"

"What other friends?" Blaze asked, sipping the tea to settle his nerves. At least the day couldn't get any worse.

Gwydion blinked at him, their lips twisting into a thoughtful little frown. "Oh, we shall have to fix that."

"Fix what?"

"I have some people you should meet!" They sprang up, not answering Blaze's question, and rushed to the door. Bakugo trotted after them, yipping happily. The door sprang open, and the witch disappeared into the hallway. A moment later, Blaze heard them knock on another door. "Yuuki, Alrik, darlings, I want you to meet someone." When they returned, it was with two dark-haired men in tow. "Blaze, this is Alrik and Yuuki. My most recent success story," they gushed.

"Your what?" Blaze frowned, eyes flicking between the two men. The shorter one with the brown eyes giggled, and the other rolled his green eyes.

"Oh, I cursed Alrik," Gwydion giggled as well. "He was a cat for almost as long as you've been around. Or maybe he's older. Hmm... was that the decade I was in Turkey or —" Gwydion broke off, their brows creasing in thought as they tried to remember.

"A cat?" Blaze snorted, trying to figure out which was which.

"Yeah, a black cat," the guy with green eyes answered. "What'd they curse you with?"

"Alrik, that's rude," the other chided gently, playfully nudging Alrik. He must be Yuuki. "You can't just ask people how they were cursed."

"Why not?" Alrik countered. "We're in the same boat, right? We should swap stories."

The two descended into soft bickering. Blaze scowled in annoyance. "Oi!" he shouted, drawing everyone's attention. "What is this shit? Gwydion's home for wayward boys? No thanks, I'm out."

"And go where?" Gwydion smirked.

Blaze's mouth opened and closed as he fumbled for a comeback. He wanted to shout, scream, curse, but Gwydion was right. He had nowhere else to go. Instead, he slumped back into the couch, looking petulant.

"That's what I thought," Gwydion said smugly. "Now, I hope you all will play nice, I've got a date!" A moment later they disappeared, leaving behind only a cloud of glitter.

"Do they do that shit all the time?" Blaze grumbled.

"You get used to it," Alrik answered with a shrug.

"Yeah, whatever." Blaze didn't want to get used to it. He didn't want to make friends. He didn't want any of this shit. But it looked like as per usual, Gwydion wasn't giving him a choice.

NINE

"I need you to take over Bakugo's care," Fable said, flopping the thin file onto Aura's desk.

Her head jerked up from where she'd been staring at the keyboard, hunt-and-pecking in a report. "Who?"

With a deep sigh, Fable removed his glasses so he could rub at the bridge of his freckled nose. This was not a conversation he particularly wanted to have, and he knew it would be just that—a *conversation*, maybe even an argument. Aura wouldn't just do as he asked and let things go. No, she would want to know why. Fable couldn't give her the full explanation, but he supposed he could give her some of it. "Blaze Ender's dog. I need you to take over his care."

"What? Why? I thought you two were getting along?" She sat up straighter, turning in her chair to look at him more closely.

There was a part of Fable—a very large part—that wanted to shout at Aura, and tell her he was not, nor would he ever, get along with that beast. He wanted to tell her what a toxic asshole Blaze was, had been for centuries now. He wanted to tell her how that bastard had killed him

—*twice*. None of that would make sense, though. So, instead, he just shook his head. "Well, we aren't," he stated.

"What did he do?" Aura's eyes narrowed in barely restrained ferocity. She had been protective of Fable since they'd met a hand full of years ago, and Fable supposed that would never go away. Then, the bumbling, gangly college student had needed her to protect him, but he didn't need that now. What he needed now was for her to not ask questions, and just take the damn file off his hands. He would not get that luxury, clearly.

Fable shrugged. "I just don't like him."

This caused Aura's eyebrows to shoot up into her bangs, a frown tugging down her pink lips. "What? Fable, you don't ever just not like someone. Did he say something? Is he mean to his dog? You guys looked like you were getting on at the bar."

The bar. That had been the beginning of the end for what could have turned into friendship, and maybe something more. Fable didn't drink usually, and the alcohol had blurred the lines between who he was now, and who he had been. "Nothing like that. The guy's just an asshole. I don't need more assholes in my life. I'm already dealing with enough. So, would you mind just doing me this solid? I know it's a lot to ask, you already have a lot of patients to handle. But I can't deal with him anymore."

Aura nodded slowly, reaching out to take the file from her desk, and look it over for a moment. "All right, I've got your back."

He smiled, shoulders relaxing ever so slightly. "Yeah, I know." Then Fable stood to leave.

"You'd tell me though, right?" Aura asked, stopping him at the door. Fable didn't turn back; he felt the tension seep back into his shoulders.

"Tell you what?"

"If he hurt you," she murmured. It didn't matter how quiet the words were, they carried so much weight that they seemed to echo off the walls lined in pictures of dogs and cats, and all manner of other creatures Aura had treated over the years.

"Of course." The lie itched at Fable's throat. He had to lie. There wasn't another choice, was there? She'd definitely have him committed if he told her he'd been cursed centuries ago to be reincarnated, so he could fight a dragon. Even more so if he told her that Blaze was that dragon.

"Good."

He nodded and left before she could ask any more questions.

THE WEATHER outside over the next couple of weeks seemed to reflect Fable's mood. As the dreary wet of early winter settled over New York, the conversation weighed heavily on Fable. He had lied to his best friend. And for what? For the sake of Blaze? To keep a secret, which was ultimately the dragon's fault? Anger—fresh and raw—bubbled low and ominous in the pit of his stomach. If he ever saw those stupidly handsome amber eyes again, he'd give that dragon a piece of his mind, damn it. He really would.

HIS CHANCE CAME on a chilly morning, as slippers with holes in the toes shuffled down the hall. Fable just needed coffee, and he was not above going out in his slippers to get it at six in the morning. Especially as his favorite little shop was right around the corner. "Mmm... I wonder if they have eggnog lattes yet," he mumbled to himself, mouth watering.

He was so caught up in his daydream of his favorite holiday treat; he didn't notice the elevator come to a stop before it was too late. Doors slid open, and then he was face to face with those amber eyes again.

"Are you shitting me?" Blaze growled, cheeks heating with ire.

Fable kept his mismatched eyes forward, not even daring to flick to the reflection of the other man in the mirrored door when it slid shut.

They rode down in silence for a long expanse of seconds, before Blaze's voice drew Fable's eyes to him. "Since when do you live here?"

Fable blinked, a frown tugging down the corners of his lips. "Since, always?" he asked, not sure why Blaze cared. *Why does it matter*, he wondered. "I was living with Aura for a while, but one of my patients told me there were some open apartments in this building, and that it was pet-friendly, so—" He shrugged. Not that it mattered. Not that any of it mattered. They weren't friends, and living in the same building didn't mean they would have to become friends. In fact, Fable was sure he could avoid Blaze easily enough if he wanted to—which he did.

"I'm going to kill that soulless bastard in their sleep," Blaze growled under his breath.

Fable blinked at him, but shook it off. They said nothing else, and Fable was grateful when the doors slid open to release him into the foyer of the building. He scurried across the gleaming tiled floor, putting as much distance as he could between himself and the irritable dragon.

IT SHOULD HAVE BEEN easy to avoid Blaze. Even if they were living in the same building, it was not a small one. There had to be a few hundred people living in the same place. So, why was it that every time Fable went down for coffee before work, Blaze grabbed the elevator at the exact same time? He wrote it off as them being on the same schedule and decided to change that. For a week, he left his apartment an hour earlier and avoided the dragon. But it seemed fate was a fickle bitch, and as she had drawn them together all of their lives, she drew them together now.

FABLE LET it slide for a while. Riding in the same elevator wasn't a big deal. They didn't have to talk, and sometimes they weren't even alone *to* talk.

"I'm not sorry," Blaze grumbled one day as he climbed into the elevator beside Fable, an overnight bag slung over his shoulder.

Fable snorted and rolled his eyes. "Then we have nothing to talk about," Fable retorted curtly. If dragons could light someone on fire with just their eyes, the glare Blaze leveled at the side of Fable's freckled face would have been enough to incinerate him. Thankfully, it was not. Nor did the look move Fable to say any more. He had written the dragon off, and that was the end of that.

"MAYBE HE'S TRYING to talk to you," Aura suggested as she stabbed her salad pointedly. "Stupid rabbit food," she grumbled when a piece of lettuce slipped off her fork from all the dressing she'd slathered it in.

"You could have just gotten a burger," Fable sighed, guilt lacing his tone.

"I made a promise," was the familiar answer. Aura had said it so many times over the years, but it never failed to remind him of that day in the doctor's office when they'd agreed to get healthier together. It felt like it was ages ago now, but still he could smell the disinfectant, and feel the bite of the cold exam table beneath his legs.

"YOU CAN'T KEEP TAKING these risks," the doctor chided softly. "Next time something like this happens to you, we may not get there in time."

"What's that mean?" Aura asked, clutching Fable's hand tighter. She'd been there every step of the way. When the paramedics had loaded him into the ambulance, when he'd woken up from surgery, when he'd had to choke down that nasty jello. And now here she was, at his follow-up visit, listening to the doctor lecture him about how little he cared for his own health.

"That means he needs to get his blood pressure under control. It's not uncommon for hypertension to accompany your condition, so you need to be careful. I can prescribe something, but it'd be better if you got this under control on your own." The doctor's words were painfully clear. Fable almost wished he would yell at him, then at least he would feel like his doctor was angry, not disappointed. Everyone knew that was way worse.

"Right, and how does he do that?" Aura continued. She had been the one asking all the questions. Fable's stomach was rolling too much to get words past the bile in his throat.

The doctor shrugged, grabbing a fresh sheet of paper to scribble stuff down. "First off, you'll need to lose some weight. Being overweight contributes significantly to this sort of thing. Next, I'd recommend more exercise and altering your diet. Try to eat as little sodium as you can, and—" The words had drifted off, becoming muffled noise in Fable's ears as he picked at the bandage where the IV had been. He'd thought after so many years of doctor visits, and IVs he would be used to this, but he wasn't. Now he doubted he ever would be.

When they left, Aura guided him towards a little café for lunch. "We're doing this together," she said as they waited in the queue behind other lunch-goers.

"Doing what together?" he asked, finally pulling himself from his daze to look at her with a bit of a frown.

"This." She wiggled the paper, and it made that strange sound that always reminded him of thunder in movies. "Eat better, exercise more, be healthier. You and me Fable, we're doing this." Fable had wanted to tell her she didn't have to. That he could do it on his own. But he knew it would be a lie; without someone to help motivate him, he'd fall back into his old habits. Instant ramen, too much coffee, not enough sleep, and heavy amounts of alcohol were practically written into the definition of being a college student.

He said nothing, he just nodded. Grateful to have someone like Aura in his life.

HE WAS STILL GRATEFUL, years later. What would he do without Aura? Where would he be? He didn't want to think about it, so he just shook his head. "I'm sorry, what were you saying?" Fable said around a mouth full of salad.

Aura sighed dramatically, dropping her fork onto the

plate so she could give Fable her undivided attention. "I was saying, maybe Blaze is trying to talk to you."

"He'll have to apologize first," Fable growled, stabbing a crouton so hard half of it went flying across the café. "Sorry," he yelped sheepishly when it landed on someone else's table. With a deep blush, he set down his own fork.

When he looked back to Aura, her expression was one of mild annoyance, with a quirked brunette brow. "Maybe he was trying to."

"Well, he hasn't said those exact words, so forget it." And that was the end of that. He wasn't going to talk about this anymore, no matter how much Aura pressed him.

FABLE GAVE Blaze no more thought over the next few weeks. Really, he didn't. He had other things to worry about. Like how the hell to find a decent gym in the city— now that it was too cold to exercise outside—that wasn't too far from either his work, or his apartment, and didn't have huge, muscular men grunting loudly. Because seriously, he didn't need that kind of negativity in his life.

He was so caught up in his search, his work, and trying out some new recipes Aura had found, that he didn't notice the mound of laundry piling up and overflowing his hamper. When it finally toppled over, nearly killing Jiji in the process, he decided it was time to do laundry.

"Who even knew I had so many clothes," he mumbled as he slung the laundry bag over his shoulder. He did his best not to stumble under the weight when the elevator gave a little jerk to head down to the basement.

With everything sorted, and loaded into separate washers, he settled in to read a book, while he waited for the machines to buzz. It was easy to lose himself in books when there was a quiet moment like this one. To blot out the world, and focus on the moving pictures inside his head. So much so, he didn't hear the *ding* of the elevator. Nor the heavy footfalls of someone joining him in the laundry room.

"Is that one of your bodice rippers?" A gruff, snarl of a voice, ripped Fable from the words on the page.

Fable's head jerked up a little too quickly, and the wobbly stool he was perched on toppled over, sending him to the floor. He reached out to catch himself on the side of the machine, his hand sliding against a piece of sharp metal that left a small but deep cut on his palm. "Shit. Shit. Shit," he cursed, pulling himself to his feet, and glaring down at the wound, as he tried to hold it shut.

Blaze was at his side in seconds, grabbing a washcloth from his own basket to press into Fable's bleeding palm. "Jeezus, that's bleeding a lot."

"I need to go upstairs," Fable panted, pressing the cloth more tightly into the wound as it quickly became soaked through. "Now."

The firefighter sprang into action; he grabbed a second cloth from his wash and pressed it into the wound. "Keep pressure on that," he ordered, then went to call the elevator again. Once it arrived, Blaze ushered Fable inside. "Floor?"

"Ten," Fable muttered, starting to feel dizzy from the blood loss. It wasn't a new sensation, but he was sure he'd never get used to it. "I left my door unlocked."

Blaze nodded, jabbing the button harder than he needed to. The only outward sign that Blaze may have been stressed by what was happening, was his fingers tapping nervously on his thigh. They rode up in silence. The room spun a little, and Fable wobbled before a large hand steadied him. Blaze stuck close after that, their arms brushing as they headed to Fable's apartment.

Once there, he nodded to the bag hanging by the door. "There's a syringe in there, grab it for me." The washcloths under his hand had gone from white, to pink, to red. It wasn't that bad; he'd certainly had worse. At least this wound didn't need stitches. But it could turn bad if he wasn't careful, he knew that well enough.

"This?" Blaze held up the clotter, and Fable nodded. "Do I need to do it?"

"No, I've got it. Can you hold the rags, though?" Blaze nodded, taking over applying pressure to the area. Fable pulled the cap off the syringe with his teeth carefully, and injected himself with the dose already prepped. "All right, now, I just need to clean it," he sighed in relief. Without a word, Blaze followed him to the sink in the bathroom, where Fable cleaned the cut carefully, first with water, and then with alcohol. Once finished, Blaze helped him to put butterfly bandages over it to hold it closed, until it healed.

"Why was it bleeding like that?" Blaze asked, finally, his words harsh from disuse, and something else Fable didn't recognize.

"Oh," Fable shrugged. "I have hemophilia."

TEN

"*I have hemophilia.*"

The words echoed over, and over again, in Blaze's mind as he finished up his laundry, sticking close to Fable in case he lost his footing again. When Fable finished with his mountain of clothes, it took everything Blaze had not to follow him upstairs.

"He doesn't need your help," Blaze chastised himself. Still, his eyes flicked to the red rags he had yet to throw in the wash.

"*I have hemophilia.*"

Fable hadn't always been sick, had he? Sure, the detection of diseases was relatively new. Still, Blaze was sure he would have noticed if the human had a bleeding disorder. They'd spent centuries chasing one another across the globe. There would have been signs. Right? No, maybe not.

And if he hadn't always been sick, what did that mean? Was there a reason, or was it sheer bad luck as a human?

"*I have hemophilia.*"

Something pitiful and ugly took up residence in the pit of Blaze's stomach. He hoped it was just bad luck. But he had to know. By the time everything was folded and loaded into the basket, Blaze had made up his mind to ask Gwydion about it.

He nudged the door shut with his hip, set the basket on the couch, and went in search of his roommate. Gwydion was in their office, sitting behind an elegant glass desk surrounded by overflowing bookshelves, their legs crossed at the ankles.

"Whatever it is, can it wait darling?" Gwydion asked, not lifting their head from where it was bent over a bright red laptop.

"No, it can't wait," Blaze said in a voice rough with emotions that he himself couldn't identify. "*I have hemophilia.*" He dropped the two washcloths he'd used to stem the flow of Fable's blood onto the smooth glass of Gwydion's desk. They landed with a soft wet *thud*.

Gwydion's head jerked up, a frown marring their features. "Are you all right? What happened? Let Auntie Gwydion see it and make it all better." Their words flew from them in a rush as they stood. Well-manicured hands already reaching out to inspect Blaze, and tend whatever wounds he may have.

"I'm fine," Blaze snarled, swatting the searching hands away. "It's not my blood."

This brought the witch up short. Their face paled, eyes blinking. "Whose—" they started and stopped to swallow worriedly. "Whose is it?"

"Fable's. But he's all right too." Blaze waved off the look of relief that washed over the witch's face. "*I have hemophilia.*" Rage simmered again, hot and threatening just below the surface of his skin. "Or as all right as someone with a bleeding disorder can be."

"Oh, that." Gwydion shrugged, returning to their seat

behind the desk.

"Yes, that." The hot anger sizzled closer to the surface now. How could Gwydion be so calm about this? This was serious, life-threatening, dangerous! For someone who seemed so hell-bent on sticking their nose where it didn't belong, it was strange to see them relax about this, as if it were nothing more than a common cold. As if it didn't matter that one of the people they had cursed was literally just one wrong move away from being broken beyond repair.

Gwydion dismissed whatever anger Blaze was feeling with a flick of their wrist. "I don't know what you want from me, Blaze."

"I want you to fix it." He smacked his hand down onto the bloody rags, causing them to disintegrate into ash.

"Do not do that to my desk," Gwydion warned. Their golden eyes fixed on his smoking hand, and only once he stood up to cross his arms over his chest did they let up. "Now, there isn't anything I can do to fix this. It's an unfortunate side effect of the spell I cast, yes, but there is no fixing it, I'm afraid. Or at least, not any fixing that *I* can do."

"Excuse me?" Blaze hissed.

Gwydion sighed, sitting back in their chair to steeple their fingers in front of them. "Fable has reincarnated into strife one too many times. Simply put, the human soul isn't meant to be torn apart and patched back together repeatedly like that. He's wearing thin."

"But he's not entirely human, he had magic that first time." Blaze's voice had gone soft as a feeling of something strange threatened to choke off his lungs. He ignored the feeling, and pressed on.

"He did, but since then, he hasn't been able to tap back into it. If he could, it would prevent any further damage."

Gwydion closed their eyes, pressing full lips to their steepled fingers in thought. "It wouldn't reverse it, but it would keep things from getting worse."

A glimmer of hope lit in Blaze's chest. This could be fixed, sort of. It wouldn't heal Fable, but it could keep him from getting sicker in future lives. "Why hasn't he been able to tap into his magic?" *And how can I help,* was the question Blaze didn't ask.

Gwydion opened their eyes and pinned Blaze with a punishing stare that rooted him to the spot. Their eyes were hard, and mouth pressed into a thin line. "That, my dear boy, is your fault. I had hoped that by this time, you two would try building each other up instead of continuing to knock each other down. The world is a different place—after all. I had hoped you'd find peace."

Blaze snorted. "Who wants peace?"

With one brow quirked, the witch rolled their golden eyes. "You do. If you don't want him to get sicker. His magic is tied to yours; if you can't get your shit together the next time, he's reborn—well, I'm not sure how bad he'll be."

Bile rose in Blaze's throat, but he forced it down. This changed nothing. "Whatever. I will not let some stupid little mage change me." He rose and turned to head back for the door, intending to ignore this situation. Fable's well-being had never been his responsibility. He silenced any thoughts that suggested otherwise.

Gwydion chuckled softly, shaking their head. "Oh, honey," their tone turned condescending, making the hair on the back of Blaze's neck stand on end. He stopped in the door to glare back at the witch over his shoulder. "You're a fool if you don't realize that he already has."

Blaze turned and slammed the door behind him. He was done talking about this.

THE FOLLOWING morning when he woke up, there was a post-it note stuck to his forehead. Pulling it away, he blinked blearily at Gwydion's flourished handwriting.

Here's a number for a supernatural therapist. I love her. Her name is Phoebe. Give her a ring when you get your head out of your ass.
XO,
Gwydion

He threw the note in the bin, not even bothering to remember the number.

WITH A LITTLE WORK, Blaze kept his distance from Fable, if not avoided him altogether.

Still, he couldn't stop thinking about the blood-soaked washcloths, and Gwydion's words. Which, led him back to the memories of Fable before it had all come crashing down. When they were almost friends.

Fable was confident and sure of himself, but still so painfully kind. Blaze wasn't sure how he'd balanced it all out, but there it was. The way his mismatched eyes softened when he'd first looked at Bakugo clung to the edges of Blaze's memories. And then there was the hard tone in Fable's voice—cut from steel—when he'd dealt with that bastard at the vet. There was little doubt, Fable was a breed all his own. But then, he always had been, and Blaze knew that.

He had to admit, after watching the young mage for

years upon years, he'd grown a little attached to him. Attached enough to want to save him from any further pain. But was it enough to want to change? That—he wasn't sure about, not yet.

Blaze was content that his luck would hold out. Maybe even until he'd moved out of the building and he wouldn't have to see Fable at the coffee shop around the corner anymore. He was all right with that, or at least he told himself he was. He didn't need to see Fable, and actually, it was probably safer for both of them if he didn't. Then he wouldn't die in strife, or whatever that nonsense was that Gwydion had spouted.

Or at least he thought his luck would hold out, until he came home to a glassy-eyed Bakugo after his shift, sometime a few weeks later.

"Hey buddy, what's wrong?" he asked softly, moving to scoop the little dog up in his arms. Baku's only response was to press his face into Blaze's shoulder with a soft exhale. "Let's get some food in you, huh? That'll make you feel better."

Blaze set the dog softly in front of his bowl, and poured some food into it. Instead of eating, the little dog just laid down, letting out another long exhale.

With a frown, Blaze sat down cross-legged on the floor. His hand moved to brush down the dog's back soothingly. "You need to eat Bakugo. You're not going to feel any better unless you do." There was no response. The dog just laid there. Blaze's teeth wore on his lip as he tried to think of what to do. He could try the soft food, but what if this wasn't that kind of issue? What if Bakugo was really sick? He pulled his phone from his pocket, and dialed before he could fully process the thought.

"Blaze, I told you—" Fable's voice answered, irritated and rough.

"I know, but I think Baku's sick, and you're close," Blaze pleaded softly. "Please. I wouldn't be calling if I wasn't worried."

Fable sighed heavily. Blaze could imagine him pulling off his glasses and rubbing the bridge of his freckled nose tiredly. "All right, I'll be down in five."

"Thank you." Blaze breathed a little easier, hanging up so he could return his attention to the little dog beside him.

By the time Fable arrived, Blaze had moved to the couch, with Bakugo sleeping soundly on a cushion beside him. He opened the door and ushered Fable inside. "So, what's the problem?" Fable asked, all-business.

"I don't know. He won't eat, and he doesn't seem like he wants to move either," Blaze sighed, wringing his hands. "I thought about making him up that nasty ass wet food, but then I didn't want to upset his stomach. So, I figured I'd just call you to make sure before I do anything to make matters worse." Was he rambling? Yes. But it had been a very long time since someone, or something, had died on Blaze. He'd somehow kept all other living creatures at bay—except Eero, but that annoying pain in the ass wasn't going anywhere, anytime soon.

"Hmm..." Fable hummed, dropping softly to his knees before the dog. His bag fell to the floor beside him, and he gently pried the dog's eyes open. Then he took Bakugo's temperature, checked his heart, and pinched the skin on his back lightly. "Hmm..." he hummed again.

By this point, Blaze was all-out pacing the room. "Well? What is it? Is he going to be okay?"

"Yeah, he should be fine," Fable nodded with a soft smile. "He's just got a bit of an upper respiratory infection, it looks like. Nothing serious. But because he can't smell the food, as before, he's not interested in it. Let's try the soft food, and see what happens. I'll give him some fluids too."

Blaze nodded, his shoulders relaxing as he let out a long breath. "Thanks, doc."

Fable moved into the kitchen without a word to heat a plate of the disgusting smelling food, and then slid it under the little dog's nose. "Come on Baku, just a little nibble," he cooed encouragingly. The dog peeked one eye open, and leaned down to take a few careful bites of the food. "There we go," Fable whispered with a smile that made Blaze feel like suddenly everything was right with the world. Had Fable always smiled like that? He couldn't remember. But it did something strange to Blaze's insides. "Much better," Fable said, petting the dog softly.

They settled into an awkward silence that Blaze was too terrified to break. What if Fable just left? Didn't Blaze want him to?

"Right then, my work here is done." Fable grinned more, standing up, and brushing his hands on his jeans.

"Uh, yeah, thanks, Doc," Blaze stuttered awkwardly, as he shifted from foot to foot. "Just add it to my tab."

Fable laughed, the sound cutting through the silence of the apartment in a tone so low, and clear, that it made Blaze's cheeks heat a little. What the hell was wrong with him? "Right, your tab." Fable shook his head, snickering more.

Fable headed for the door without another word, and Blaze moved to follow, only half realizing what he was doing. When they made it there, Fable turned towards him, and quirked one dark brow in question. But Blaze's brain had long since disconnected from the rest of his body. He dipped his head, and pressed his lips to Fable's in a soft, sweet kiss.

The shorter man stiffened under the kiss. Then a moment later, he shoved Blaze away, reared back with his left arm, and punched Blaze with everything he had, across the jaw. Distantly, Blaze heard the door slam, and when he regained full cognizance, pain bloomed along his jaw. "That's gonna leave a mark," he mumbled.

DESPITE BLAZE'S BEST EFFORT, he couldn't get the kiss out of his mind. The bruise that had bloomed on his jaw probably didn't help. No, it definitely didn't help. For every time he pulled on a shirt, or slung his fireproof jacket over his shoulders, he brushed the bruised skin, and it stung. It was a constant reminder.

He pressed his fingers into the darkened skin with one hand, while the other unlocked the apartment door. The image of Fable—eyes aflame with anger, cheeks tinged pink under his freckles, and lips hanging open in shock—flashed through his mind for perhaps the hundredth time. So caught up in these thoughts was he, that he didn't notice the pile of shoes beside the front door, and only belatedly realized that there were three men lounging on his living room sofa after they trapped him with them.

"What the flying frack do you idiots want?" Blaze asked, eyes flicking from Yuuki, to Alrik, to finally land on Eero. Eero's face was lit in a wide, mischievous smile. That wasn't good. That was never good.

"This is an intervention, man," Eero chirped cheerfully. He rose from the couch to clap Blaze on the shoulder, before shoving him into a chair.

"I don't need an intervention." Blaze bared his teeth,

crossing his arms over his chest, and staring hard at Eero. He willed the redhead's hair to catch on fire from his gaze alone. It didn't work; it never did.

"Then where is the bruise from?" Alrik smirked, resting his chin on his palm, as he leaned on the arm of the sofa.

Blaze lifted his chin, vowing not to talk. If they wanted to host an intervention, so be it. He didn't have to take part.

"And while we're on the topic, let's talk about how you keep calling Fable to come look after your dog." Eero added with a chuckle; flopping down beside Yuuki.

"Yeah, so?" Blaze countered petulantly.

"You can't keep doing that," Yuuki spoke up finally, but he didn't look up from where he was wringing his hands in his lap. He looked like the other two had dragged him into this, and he wasn't entirely comfortable with it. But that didn't stop Blaze from fixing him with an angry stare.

"And why not?" Blaze knew why not, he didn't really need the answer, but he asked anyways. He would not make this easy on them, not at all.

"It's rude," Eero chimed in. "He's not your personal veterinarian."

"And selfish," Alrik added.

"Right, and selfish." Eero nodded in agreement.

"Shouldn't there be snacks? I thought interventions had snacks," Blaze snarked back at them, hoping to throw them off balance.

"You can have snacks after you've answered our questions," Yuuki said firmly. He finally lifted his brown eyes to meet Blaze's glare head on. A look of quiet determination had set into the chef's face, and Blaze had to admit, he admired it. It reminded Blaze of Fable. "Where did the bruise come from?"

Blaze muttered something unintelligible, half hoping they wouldn't ask again.

No such luck. "I'm sorry, what was that?" Eero held a hand up to cup his ear. "Repeat it for me."

"I kissed Fable," Blaze huffed, lifting his chin to glare at the corner of the room. He was not blushing. He most certainly was not blushing.

"I'm sorry, you did what now?" Eero's brows knitted in confusion. "I must be hearing things. I thought you just said that you kissed Fable."

"He did say he kissed Fable," Yuuki confirmed softly, his eyes still fixed on Blaze.

"No, that can't be right." Eero laughed, shaking his head. "Because that would be the most asshole thing he could pull at this point. And surely, he's not that stupid."

"Well, maybe that's why he's got a bruise now." Alrik snorted, green eyes dancing with mirth.

"Yeah, he punched me." Blaze's eyes fell to the floor in guilt, his hand lifting to scrub at the back of his head. It had been a stupid thing to do. Rash. Impulsive. And he'd paid for it.

Eero and Alrik both broke out into uproarious laughter, only growing louder when Blaze lifted his head to scowl at them. "Come on you two, let's not be mean," Yuuki scolded, but it did nothing to stop them.

After a few minutes the laughter died out, Alrik's eyes were glassy, and Eero was clutching his stomach. "What's your next move?" Eero asked through a wheeze.

Blaze shrugged.

"You don't have one," Alrik supplied flatly. It wasn't a question, it was a statement of fact, and Alrik was right. Blaze didn't have one, and he was pitiful.

"Gwydion said they suggested a therapist," Yuuki offered. "Maybe start there?"

Eero nodded in agreement. "It can't hurt."

BLAZE AGREED BEGRUDGINGLY, and made an appointment for the following week.

The waiting room was empty when he showed up half an hour early for his appointment, so he busied himself with a car magazine. He did his best to focus on words like 'pistons' and 'horsepower', when all he really wanted was to bolt before the door could open. Blaze knew he needed to do this; he knew he had no choice. But that didn't mean he had to like it. Before he could chicken out entirely, the door opened, and a teenager with bright eyes trotted out.

"Thanks again, Doctor Slaine. It was nice talking to you," the young girl said, bouncing on her toes a little, as if she'd take off at any given moment. Those eyes flicked around the room, flickering yellow when they landed on Blaze.

Werewolf, Blaze's brain supplied, but he kept his mouth shut.

"As I said before, Timber, please call me Phoebe. No need for this Doctor Slaine business," the blonde woman answered, laughing softly.

"Right. Phoebe," Timber said the name slowly as if perhaps she were tasting it, and trying to decide if it sounded odd, or not. After a moment, the girl shook her head, laughing. "Nah, I'll stick to Doctor Slaine."

Phoebe laughed, nodding. "All right, then. I'll see you next week." Timber nodded, and headed out with only a glance over her shoulder at Blaze. Once the door to the hall shut, Phoebe looked to him. Calculating blue eyes searched Blaze for some understanding. Blaze shifted uncertainly under her knowing gaze. "Blaze Ender."

"Yeah, that's me." Blaze nodded, feeling awkward and unsure if she even meant for him to answer.

"I'm Phoebe, come on in." She motioned over her shoulder and then turned to head into her office again. Blaze rose quickly to follow her. Inside was a chair and a comfy-looking couch. Phoebe took up residence in the chair and gestured to the sofa. "Please, have a seat, Mr. Ender."

"I think I'll stand, thanks." Blaze shrugged, crossing his arms over his chest, and leaning against the arm of the couch instead of sitting on it.

With one blonde brow quirked, Phoebe looked down at the file perched on her crossed legs for a moment. "Gwydion referred you to me, right?"

Blaze nodded, almost afraid that talking would give him away. Maybe it would.

"We don't have to talk, Mr. Ender, if you aren't ready. Just coming here today is a good first step. We can work up to talking." Her voice was so serene, it caught Blaze off guard. His eyes flicked up to meet blue eyes, calm like the ocean after a storm. Smooth, and free from ripples. "We'll move at your pace here."

"I'm not a coward," Blaze blurted without a second thought. He wasn't sure why, or where those words had come from. But some vague, angry part of himself felt that that's what she was implying. That he was too scared to admit his faults.

"No, of course not," Phoebe conceded, a soft smile on her lips. "You've already proven yourself braver than most by coming here to talk to me. Most people can't even take that step."

Blaze nodded curtly in reply, pressing his lips together.

"So, if we aren't going to talk about your past, perhaps we can talk about what brought you here? Gwydion didn't give me any information, they just said that one of their charges would come by to see me today." Phoebe's eyes fixed on him again, pinning him to the spot.

"I have—" he started, and then swallowed roughly after a moment, before starting over. "I have anger issues."

Phoebe nodded, scribbling something down without pulling her eyes away from him. "And you've come to me searching for a means to control your temper?"

"Yes. I was hoping you could teach me to squeeze a stress ball, or snap a rubber band, or whatever it is humans do to control their temper." He chuckled to himself, knowing how ridiculous it sounded. A dragon with a stress ball.

Phoebe snorted despite herself. "I'm sorry, I'm not laughing at you."

"It sure as shit sounds like you're laughing at me." Blaze glared.

"No, it's just—you think a stress ball will unravel centuries of trauma?" Phoebe swallowed down her laughter, forcing an impassive look onto her face.

The question stumped him. Blaze blinked at her, a frown tugging at the corners of his lips. "No, I guess not," he whispered, feeling like an idiot.

"It's all right, Blaze. I understand you want a quick fix. Everyone who comes here does, they think that because I've been in the business since before it *was* a business, I can just fix them with a snap of my fingers. But it doesn't work that way. The supernatural, just like our human counterparts, have complex emotions. Maybe even more so, when one has lived as long as you have. There is no quick fix. We have to unpack all of it," her tone was calm and steady.

"That will take forever," Blaze huffed. "I don't have forever."

With a quirked brow, she nodded. "All right then, I can teach you some simple exercises to help you control your temper while we do the work. But you have to continue to do the work," she warned. "Can you do that?"

Blaze chewed on the inside of his cheek, thinking. "What does that mean?"

"That means coming here once a week and calling me whenever you feel you're slipping. I know your type; you don't like to ask for help. But if this is going to work, you have to have the courage to call me when you feel you can't do it on your own. You can't walk out that door and ghost me. Are we clear?" Phoebe's tone was gentle, but stern. Blaze admired her for that, just as he admired Fable for it.

Blaze nodded slowly.

"I need to hear you say it, Mr. Ender. I need to hear you say that you understand," her words were still soft.

"I understand," he grumbled softly, with a nod.

"Excellent." She smiled, sitting back a little in her chair. "Let's get started. I'll give you some techniques you can try, and we'll figure out which works best over the next week. These are by no means one size fits all, but I want to make sure you have the tools you need to conquer this."

"Will it involve a rubber band or some shit?"

Phoebe laughed, shaking her head. "No, no rubber band. That technique is largely fictional, and when used it's for compulsive behavior. You aren't compulsive, are you?"

Blaze took a moment to think about himself, and his reactions to things. "Impulsive, not compulsive."

Phoebe nodded. "Let's try counting to ten, first. Next

time you feel angry enough to snap, take a moment, and count to ten. This will give you a few extra seconds to assess your emotions, and see if you are reacting appropriately to the situation."

THE FIRST TIME he had to count to ten ironically—or unironically, depending on how you were looking at it—came but an hour later. Blaze was standing in line, waiting for his coffee and someone cut in front of him.

"Oi! Jackass!" Blaze's angry voice broke the soft rumble of conversation in the shop.

She spun to meet his eyes; black brows raised. She couldn't have been more than fourteen, and was popping her gum loudly. "Yeah? What ya want, old man?" *Pop!*

A snarl rose on his lips, hands fisting and growing warm with rage. He opened his mouth to bark back at her, but snapped it shut a moment later. A little voice in the back of his head—that sounded strangely like Phoebe—whispered, *'Take a breath. Count to ten.'*

So he did. He took a deep breath and counted. And by the time he reached five, he realized this wasn't worth it. All this would earn him was a permanent ban from one of the best coffee shops in the neighborhood. This child wasn't worth that. "Nah, you go ahead." He shrugged, tucking his hands into his pockets.

Pop! The girl turned back around to order her basic bitch coffee, and trotted off without a word.

The whole experience left Blaze feeling both strangely exhausted, and uplifted. He'd done it. He'd controlled himself enough to not snap at someone, and light something on fire. Progress. Finally!

ELEVEN

Fable, too, couldn't seem to get the kiss out of his head. He hadn't wanted it, and he'd shown his displeasure. He had the bruised knuckles to prove it. Still, it lingered in the back of his mind, for some strange reason. It hadn't been unpleasant—Fable would be a liar, if he said that it was. Blaze was very handsome, and he kissed earnestly. The kiss hadn't been the problem; it was all the other *stuff* that was. Their shared history, and unfinished business. Perhaps, if Blaze had apologized before planting one on him, Fable wouldn't have punched him. Fable supposed they'd never know now.

"Hey, your turn," someone behind him whispered softly, pulling Fable from his thoughts.

"Oh, right. Thanks." He turned to offer the young man a warm smile, before moving to the counter to place his order. He pulled his wallet from the bag on his shoulder, opening it to pull out his card.

"Oh no, your order was already paid for," the girl behind the counter chirped, her smiled bright and mischievous.

Fable blinked, frowning a little. "What?"

"You're Fable Alperen, right?" she asked, looking back down at a piece of receipt paper that had indecipherable scribble on it.

"Uh, yeah?"

She smiled more. "Thought so, he said you had heterochromia and freckles, and there's only one person who comes in here like that."

"Who said?"

"That cute, angry firefighter who always comes in here. What was his name, Jen?" She turned to the other girl who was jotting Fable's name onto a cup.

"I dunno, he didn't say." Jen shrugged.

"Right." Fable shifted awkwardly, returning his wallet to his bag. "Umm... thanks?"

"Don't thank us. He paid for it," replied the first girl whose name tag was a scribbled mess, but it looked like it started with a C? Maybe Crystal? "And just a tip," Maybe-Crystal said, leaning over the register so she could whisper to him. "I'd lock that shit down if I were you. He's hella hot."

Fable flushed brightly. "I'll keep that in mind. Do I just —" He gestured to the pickup counter.

Maybe-Crystal nodded. "Jen will be done with your order shortly. Have a nice day!" she warbled cheerfully with a wink.

Fable shuffled over to the pickup counter, trying to ignore the heat that settled under his scarf as he waited for his coffee. He felt like every pair of eyes was on him when he snagged the cup, sipping it slowly. "Thanks," he mumbled. Then ducked his head and shuffled back out into the cold—hand clutched tightly around his gifted coffee.

THE FOLLOWING morning it happened again. And again, the day after that. By Friday, he had only paid for his coffee once. He half expected it to stop by the following week, and wasn't sure if he'd find that disappointing or preferable. On the one hand, it felt weird not paying for his morning order, especially when he wasn't even on speaking terms with Blaze. But on the other, it was nice to be thought of.

It didn't stop. Three weeks went by in this fashion, and the girls behind the counter were so used to it that they had his order ready for him when he walked in. It was strange—nice, but strange.

"MAYBE HE'S TRYING TO APOLOGIZE," Yuuki said, looking up from the pot where he was working on his famous ramen broth.

Alrik snorted from his perch on a stool at the counter. "It'll take a lot more than some coffee to apologize for what he did throughout the centuries."

Fable sighed, scrubbing at his face. It felt strange to talk about his curse with someone. Even weirder with someone who used to be one of his furry patients. The whole conversation felt like an episode of the Twilight Zone, and Fable still wasn't sure how all of it had come up to begin with. Not that it mattered. It was nice to have someone to talk with about all of this magical nonsense, without having to worry they would call him crazy.

"But isn't it a good sign that he's trying, at least?" Yuuki frowned softly, shaking his head. "I mean, come on, Alrik, that's got to mean something."

"Yeah, because a couple coffees can clearly make up for killing someone. Twice." Alrik rolled his eyes, picking up a dry ramen noodle to flick at Yuuki.

"Don't waste food," Yuuki chided, pinning Alrik with a glare that made the green-eyed man flush.

"You were a cat for centuries," Fable started, breaking the silence of their staring match.

"Yeah." Alrik shrugged. "So?"

"So, what was it like watching people around you just —" Fable frowned, realizing belatedly that the question may have been a touch insensitive.

"Die?" Alrik finished for him, and Fable nodded. Alrik sighed, running a hand through his black hair. "At some point, you become detached from it all. Like you aren't human anymore. But let's be real here, Blaze never *was* human."

"If anything," Yuuki chimed in. "Living amongst humans for centuries has made him more human. Honestly, he seems like a good guy to me."

"You think everyone is a good guy," Alrik pointed out.

"Stop being argumentative," Yuuki grumbled, turning back to the pot and grabbing a spoonful. "And taste this." He held the spoon out to Alrik, and the other man carefully slurped up the broth before nodding his approval.

"I'm not trying to be argumentative," Alrik responded after swallowing.

"You are," Fable agreed with Yuuki.

"Look, I'm just playing devil's advocate here. Yuuki would be gung-ho to forgive and forget. He's just that sort of person—"

"That's why you love me," Yuuki interrupted.

"Yes, it is," Alrik agreed before continuing on. "But that's not the point. The point is—Yuuki is a sweet guy, but you didn't come here for mushy, romantic, idealistic advice."

"I didn't come here for advice at all," Fable pointed out.

"And since you didn't come here for that kind of advice," Alrik continued on as if Fable hadn't spoken. "One of us has to be the voice of reason."

"Then what do you suggest?" Yuuki asked, dumping vegetables into the broth to cook, before moving to the fridge to pull out three eggs. "Just ignore him, and hope he goes away?"

"Hardly." Alrik rolled his eyes, a smile tugging up the beautiful lilt of his thin lips. "Make him work for it."

"I'm sorry?" Fable blinked; brows pulled together in confusion. "Isn't that what he's doing with the coffee?"

"The coffee is a start, but if he wants to prove he's changed, you both have to stop avoiding each other."

"I haven't been avoiding him," Fable protested weakly. But he had, he'd changed his schedule to make sure they weren't in the same place at the same time. He even started paying for cabs to get into work, instead of taking the subway, so he could leave later.

"It's not entirely your fault, he's been avoiding you too." Yuuki laughed softly.

"Honestly, you both are so obvious, it's a wonder Gwydion hasn't caught onto this tom-foolery." Alrik gestured with a wiggle of his fingers.

"Who says tom-foolery anymore?" Fable teased.

But Alrik would not be derailed. "Let yourself run into him. See how things go. If he's still the same jerk, then you can go back to avoiding each other. Maybe you'll get lucky and he'll move out soon."

"And how would you propose we stop avoiding one another?"

"Leave that to us." Yuuki winked mischievously. Fable wasn't sure he liked the sound of that, but he decided not to protest. It wouldn't do him any good anyway. It seemed his two friends had made up their minds about the whole thing.

THE NEXT MORNING when Fable went down for his coffee, he went at his usual time, instead of leaving late. When he walked into the little coffee shop, and didn't immediately spot the taller man's strawberry blond hair in the line, he thought he might have gotten away with it. That things would continue on as they had been. That he, and Blaze, would continue to just miss one another, until Blaze moved out of the building. Fable was almost disappointed at the thought.

"What do you mean you're out of chai?" An all too familiar angry voice said from the front of the line. Scratch that, he was definitely not disappointed. He could go his entire life without ever hearing that angry voice again, and be perfectly happy.

"I'm sorry, sir. Our shipment didn't come in this morning, and we're out of a lot of things," Maybe-Crystal answered in a tone that quivered just a little at the end.

Fable peeked around the tall man in front of him to get a view of Blaze's back. The fireman's shoulders were stiff with tension beneath his black leather jacket, and his hair hidden beneath a knit beanie. That must be why Fable hadn't noticed him at first.

"Well, then—" Blaze growled, but cut off his own angry tirade before it could get any further. Fable watched in wonder as Blaze ducked his head, taking a deep breath that was so loud Fable could hear it some feet away. After a few seconds, he exhaled noisily again. "I understand. Can I just pay for my friend's drink then?" The words that left him now were softer, more controlled than Fable had ever heard him.

"Of course, sir. Again, I'm sorry for the inconvenience," Maybe-Crystal answered with the best customer-service-smile Fable had ever seen.

And then Blaze said something that rocked Fable to his core. "No need to apologize, it's not your fault. I'm sorry for getting testy with you."

"No worries! Your total is 5.99," she chirped, the smile never slipping.

"Actually," Fable piped up, ducking under the stanchion to get to the front of the line. "Don't bother, I'm here, and I can pay for my own. And while we're at it, do you guys still have the pumpkin spice?"

Maybe-Crystal's smile slipped from customer-service-ready to something more genuine, and she nodded. "Yes, we do."

"Wonderful, he'll take a small one of those, and my regular." Fable pulled his wallet from his pocket, doing his best to ignore the stunned silence of the tall firefighter beside him. He turned to head back to the pickup counter, and Blaze followed along silently.

When Blaze found his tongue again, what he said was, "I'm not a basic bitch."

Fable giggle-snorted loud enough that Jennifer—making the drinks—looked up at him curiously. He shook his head, and she looked back to her work. "You sure about that?"

Blaze scowled a little, eyes narrowing on Fable, but he didn't say anything.

"Okay, first of all, Pumpkin Spice is delicious and no amount of furry-boot-wearing pre-teens will convince me otherwise. Secondly, it has a lot of the same ingredients as Chai tea," Fable said reasonably, a teasing grin still on his features.

"Yeah, okay," Blaze grunted.

"Just trust me on this, yeah?" Fable held the small cup out to him, one brow quirked. "Besides, if you don't like it, at least you didn't pay for it. Right?"

"Yeah, I guess." Blaze took the cup, blowing on it through the little sipper hole for a moment. Then he took a careful sip, his nose wrinkled in concentration as he considered the flavor on his tongue. The expression was *almost* cute—if Fable were into that sort of thing. Which he wasn't. A soft smile turned up the corners of Blaze's lips, and he pulled the cup back from his mouth.

"Well?" Fable asked, grabbing his own coffee to take a happy sip.

"It's not as good as my Chai, but it'll do in a pinch," Blaze conceded, the little smile still on his lips. "Thanks for this." The words flowed more easily from his lips now than they had the first time Blaze had thanked him. As if perhaps he'd become accustomed to saying them.

"You're welcome."

"Right," Blaze said awkwardly, taking another sip from his cup as if he needed something to do with his hands. "I've gotta get to the station. I'll–um- I'll see you around."

"Yeah, see you," Fable answered, unable to hold off a little smirk at the blush that crept onto Blaze's cheeks. "Maybe I'll see you on laundry day."

"Yeah, maybe."

SHARING a few minutes every morning as they sipped their coffee before heading into work, became a regular part of Fable's routine. Most of the time, not more than a 'thanks' passed between them, but sometimes they had full conversations. Fable would admit it was nice. Over the weeks that passed, he learned a lot about Blaze. That dragons didn't feel the effects of caffeine the same way humans did, which is why Blaze preferred tea. And that Blaze hated the cold, but he'd moved to New York because of Eero, who had fallen in love with Central Park when it was first being built.

These little tidbits added up to create the image of a person. Blaze sounded less, and less, like the beast Fable had once known, and more like a regular guy.

"DO you always wait until your laundry nearly kills your cat to do it?" Blaze asked. A little smirk tugged at the corner of his lips as he eyed Fable.

Fable shrugged, pulling a pair of pants from the dryer to fold them, before laying them in the basket atop the nearby machine. "I've been busy."

Blaze snorted softly, but didn't argue. They sat in silence for a few minutes, as Fable pulled more clothes from the dryer to fold them neatly. Then he started pulling out socks, dropping those off to the side of one neat stack of clothes. "Wait. Are you not going to match your socks?" Blaze asked, incredulously.

Fable looked up, and laughed, shaking his head. "No, of course not. I hardly ever wear matching socks." He lifted his pants legs to show off one grey, and one green sock, tucked into his worn slippers.

"You're a monster!" Blaze gasped in shock.

"Hardly. At worst, I'm chaotic good." Fable shrugged, grabbing another hand full of socks to throw into the basket with the others.

"Bullshit. You're chaotic neutral at best." Blaze's tone was teasing, light. Unlike Fable had ever heard it before. There was something playful in the way this conversation was going, and Fable realized they hadn't spoken like this ever.

"Please, only boring people pair their socks," Fable offered with a playful eye roll.

"No, *adults* pair their socks." Blaze chuckled softly. It was a nice laugh, Fable realized. Soft and warm. Happy, in a way Fable hadn't thought Blaze could be.

"Who wants to be an adult anyhow?" Fable countered, leaning in close as if challenging him and stuffing more socks into the basket—unpaired.

Blaze blinked, flustered by their sudden closeness. Fable could see a soft flush painting the fireman's cheeks. He wondered idly if all dragons could blush, or just red ones. "I guess no one," Blaze finally responded lamely.

TWELVE

*H*e *was so close*, Blaze thought, still blushing as he remembered the feeling of Fable's soft laughter fanning out over his lips. *Too close.*

All Blaze had wanted to do in that moment was kiss Fable—again. Which he was sure would not be appreciated —again.

"But how do you know he wouldn't have appreciated it?" Phoebe asked, pulling Blaze from his reverie.

"Because last time I did something like that, he punched me in the face," Blaze answered, frustration lacing every word.

"Yes, but that was almost two months ago. Since then, you've made great strides to prove you've changed. You've been able to control your temper, and it even seems like perhaps you two have become friends." Her words were simple, logical, even true, as always.

"It's not enough," Blaze argued.

"Why isn't it?" Clear blue eyes swept over him, examining him like a scientist would a test subject. "You've apologized to him, haven't you?"

Blaze lifted his head from where he'd been glaring at his fingers with narrowed amber eyes. "What?"

"Well, you apologized. So, you should be able to move towards—"

"I never apologized," Blaze cut her off, frowning to himself. "I never said I was sorry for what happened." In fact, he'd done the exact opposite.

Phoebe frowned, her nose scrunching up. With a deep sigh, she ran a hand through her straight blonde hair, and squeezed her eyes shut as if perhaps Blaze were testing her insurmountable patience. He probably was. He could never tell exactly what his therapist thought when they talked. "You moron," she said tiredly.

"I don't think you're supposed to call your patients morons," Blaze argued, no real bite in his tone. It was hard to be mad at someone who over the last few weeks had listened to him lay himself bare. Phoebe knew all there was to know of Blaze Ender, and to be honest, Blaze felt a certain peace knowing he wasn't alone in it anymore. She knew about the young men who had sought to prove themselves by slaying a dragon, and would cut off bits and pieces of him, leaving his body littered in scars. He'd told her about the guilt that rested deep in the pit of his stomach when he remembered what he'd done to Fable. Even how, at some point, he'd thought maybe he and Fable could be friends, early on, before he'd killed the mage. So, he valued her words and advice above all others.

A snort left the woman as she shook her head, before fixing him with another tired look. "No, I suppose not. But seriously? All this time you've been trying to make it up to him, and you didn't even do the most important part?"

Blaze shrugged, scrubbing at the back of his neck anxiously. "I'm not good with words."

A small smiled tugged up the corner of Phoebe's lips. "I understand that, but you are much better with your words than you used to be. Just remember the techniques I taught you. Whenever you struggle to express yourself, you—" she let her words drift off, waiting for him to fill in the blanks.

"Close my eyes, take a breath, and speak slowly," he repeated the words she'd said to him over, and over, studiously. "I know."

"Exactly." Phoebe nodded approvingly. "Trust me on this, you'll get much further with him if you actually tell him how you're feeling. Not all people can read actions the way we older beings can. They need to be told."

"And how do you suggest I tell him?" Blaze grumbled, running a hand through his strawberry blond hair, mussing it more than usual.

Phoebe was silent for a few moments, looking thoughtful. When she finally spoke, she said, "Well, if someone had killed me—"

"That was an accident," Blaze argued, but she waved him off.

"I'd at least want an apology dinner. Why not ask your new friends to help?"

WHICH IS HOW—DESPITE his better judgement— Blaze found himself knocking on Yuuki and Alrik's door that evening. Thinking over the words he'd needs to say over, and over, mumbling them under his breath.

Alrik opened the door, brows lifted high enough to disappear into his black bangs. "Blaze?"

"I need help," Blaze rushed the words out before he could choke on them.

"Come inside," Alrik said, not hesitating to step out of the way and let the dragon into his and Yuuki's small apartment. That alone was a testament to how frazzled he must have looked, Alrik wasn't giving him shit.

"What do you need?" Yuuki asked, his hand still held up where it had paused whatever show they'd been watching together.

Blaze felt his shoulders tense. A small, angry voice in his head lashed out. Called him weak. Told him he didn't need help. Least of all from some human, and a pansy prince. But he bit down on his cheek until the voice fell silent and then said, "I need to plan an apology dinner for Fable."

WHAT HAD SURPRISED Blaze most about Alrik and Yuuki wasn't how good Yuuki was at teaching, or how willing Alrik was to act as a taste tester. It was that they both had jumped to help him without a second thought. Here were two men who he had only known a hand full of months. Who he hadn't been very kind to. Humans! And they had leaped at the chance to help their friend without so much as a 'what's in it for me?' Blaze had never thought of humans as being willing to help another human, much less a dragon. But these two knew what he was, and they had helped anyway.

"Maybe you were wrong about humanity all these years," Gwydion whispered as if reading his thoughts. They snatched a vegetable from the neat stack on the board that Blaze was using to chop and sort.

"Don't eat my ingredients." Blaze swatted their hand away, ignoring the look of annoyance that crossed the witch's face. "I need all of it."

"These are just toppings." Gwydion pouted petulantly. "You don't need that exact amount." But when Blaze cut them a look, Gwydion relented. "Oh, all right. How did you get Fable to agree to this, anyway?"

Blaze shrugged. "I just asked if he'd like to come by for dinner. We're on friendlier terms now, he even seemed excited."

"And then you promised to make Pide?"

A flush stained Blaze's cheeks, and he ducked his head back down to the dough he was working on. "He said he hadn't eaten anything from his homeland since he moved to New York. Apparently, his mom is Turkish."

"Hmm..." Gwydion hummed, leaning back on their heels. "Funny how that works sometimes."

"Don't you have someplace to be?" Blaze asked, a note of irritation lacing his tone. Gwydion merely shrugged in response. "You've got about ten minutes to make yourself scarce. I don't need you hovering over me while we do this."

"Do what?" Gwydion smirked, leaning forward to press their palms onto the countertop. "You planning to kiss him again?"

Blaze growled, throwing a piece of pepper at Gwydion's face.

The witch laughed, scurrying off. "Don't do anything I wouldn't!" They wiggled their fingers from their office doorway and disappeared inside.

"You heard me, witch. Make yourself scarce!" Blaze shouted. He returned to kneading the dough a little harder perhaps than he ought. He could hear Yuuki in the back of his mind reminding him not to overwork it. He began rolling out the dough of the Pide right before there was a knock on the door.

"I'll get it," Gwydion called, trotting across their shared

living space in a long-sleeved velvet dress they hadn't been wearing a moment ago. Blaze resisted the urge to snarl, forcing himself to focus on the dough instead. "Ah! Fable! How nice to see you again!" Blaze heard Gwydion's bright voice from the direction of the door, and he gritted his teeth.

"You look nice, Gwydion," Fable complimented, a smile in his voice. "Am I underdressed?"

"Oh no, darling. I was just on my way out. I've got a big date. Huge. With a sweet little nurse, he's probably waiting for me downstairs as we speak. But you two have fun." Gwydion's words were so smooth, Blaze couldn't tell if they were lying, or not. Perhaps the witch did have a date after all. "Behave yourself, Blaze dear," Gwydion called into the kitchen in a teasing lilt.

"Never," Blaze teased back, a little smile tugging at his lips.

Gwydion giggled loudly. "He's in the kitchen. I'll see you boys later." Then Blaze heard the door open and shut once more, and the witch was gone.

"So, uh, can I help with anything?" Fable asked as he entered the kitchen. "I'm not a great cook, but I've been told I make a pretty good sous chef."

"Well, that's a ringing endorsement if I've ever heard one," Blaze replied sarcastically, but there was laughter on his tongue.

Fable shrugged, smirking. "Take it, or leave it."

Blaze looked at him for a long moment—as if seriously considering his offer, and then nodded. "Start putting together that one with whatever you like on it," he instructed, pointing to a small round piece of dough.

Fable's eyes grew wide, making them look even more startlingly beautiful. "You made Pide dough?"

Blaze nodded.

"Like from scratch?"

Blaze nodded again.

"That's so amazing!" Excitement heated Fable's freckled cheeks.

Blaze shrugged, his own cheeks warming at the praise. "Whatever, just make up yours so I can get it folded and in the oven."

"Yeah. I will." Fable laughed happily, beginning to pile his dough with cheese and vegetables. They worked in companionable silence as they made up two Pide each before Blaze slipped them into the oven to cook.

"So, you don't cook?" Blaze asked, leaning against the counter to watch the window to the oven for the telltale signs of browning dough.

"Oh, I cook." Fable snickered, scrubbing a hand through his curly brown hair, and making it that much more unruly. "I'm just not sure it's anything I'd want to serve another person."

"That bad, huh?" Blaze teased softly.

"It's edible, if that's what you mean. It's just not very tasty." Fable shrugged. "I suppose I should be better about it, since—you know."

Blaze's brows creased in confusion. "What?"

Fable sighed, shoulders slumping a little. "An unfortunate side effect of hemophilia is hyper-tension. If I'm not careful with my health, my blood pressure goes through the roof. Which only makes the bleeding more dangerous. So, I've been on a strict diet since college. I uh—" Fable broke off, wearing on his pale lower lip in thought. As if he wasn't sure if he should say the next part or not. After less than a moment of indecision, he made up his mind. "I had a pretty big spill when I was in college. I'd gone out drinking with my girlfriend at the time—not Aura—and she just kept goading me into it. She always said I was too uptight when I was sober," he shrugged, a frown creasing his brow at the memory. "So, she preferred me wasted or high. Anyway, I stumbled into something. A table? Maybe. I don't really remember, I was so blackout drunk. The next thing I remember, I'm waking up in the ambulance with Aura sobbing her eyes out beside me."

"Where was your girlfriend?" Blaze asked, reasonably sure he didn't want to know the answer to the question.

Fable snorted. "She couldn't be bothered. Riding to the hospital with me would cut into her party time."

"What a bitch," Blaze grumbled, heat lacing his tone, and insides, at the thought of someone doing that to Fable.

"Yeah, I mean, she was." Fable shook his head, as if clearing away the cobwebs. "I guess that's what I liked about her. I kind of had a thing for people who treated me like dirt. Got me why. Anyway, after that, they found out I had hypertension. I was twenty, and I had an issue usually reserved for middle-aged people. So, Aura and I agreed to eat better together."

Blaze nodded but said nothing as he kept his eyes focused on the food in the oven. A part of him wanted to see the expression on Fable's face right then, but another part was terrified what he'd see if he looked up.

"That's also when I decided I needed to cut toxic people out of my life. I couldn't afford to let someone like her influence my decisions again if I wanted to live to achieve my goals." There was a calm, resolute tone to Fable's voice. As if he'd come to terms with all of this and that was that.

Blaze didn't know what to say to that, so he stayed quiet, watching the dough turn golden and the cheese melt. "I think they're done," he breathed when the silence got to be too much.

Fable slipped off the chair and moved to peek in through the oven window. "They look delicious!"

Blaze grunted, grabbing the oven mitts—he most certainly did not need, but Yuuki had insisted on—from beside him on the counter, and moving to pull the tray out. With a too-big spatula, that magically appeared beside the pan, he slid them onto a platter, and headed for the table.

Fable flopped down in his chair across from Blaze, eyes fixed on the Pide in front of him. "They smell even better!"

Blaze flushed a little smile on his lips. "Eat up."

Silence reigned once more, as the two men served themselves, and ate happily. Yuuki had told Blaze not to worry if things were quiet at first. He'd said that quiet enjoyment was the sign of a good meal. So, Blaze did his best not to shift awkwardly in his seat as they ate.

"I need to say something—" Blaze started.

"I need to ask you something—" Fable said at the exact same time.

They both laughed for a moment, shaking their heads.

"You first," Blaze offered.

"No, please, you go ahead," Fable insisted.

Blaze nodded, setting down his fork, and taking a deep breath. He had thought about this speech over, and over, for the last four months. How did one apologize not just for a lifetime of pain, but for *several* lifetimes of it? "I uh." He swallowed roughly. "I'm sorry, for–for everything. And you don't have to forgive me, I know much of what I've done is unforgivable. But I just wanted you to know how deeply I regret—all of it."

"Oh, I know," Fable answered, a teasing little grin on his face.

"You know?" Blaze asked, disbelief and irritation lacing his tone.

Fable shrugged, the grin spreading further. "Yeah, three weeks of coffee without so much as a word kind of gave me a hint. I mean, I appreciate that you've finally said it. I know how hard it is for you to admit you were wrong. But I've known you feel guilty about what happened for a while now."

"And?" Blaze prompted, his heart racing in his chest. If Fable knew, but hadn't said, did that mean he didn't forgive Blaze? Was all of this for naught?

"And I forgive you," Fable answered, silencing the panicked voice that had begun to rattle off possibilities in Blaze's mind.

Blaze nodded in astonishment. Almost—*almost*—forgetting that Fable too had asked something. "What did you want to ask?"

"Oh," Fable remembered, a little flush settling under his freckles again. "Would you mind teaching me how to use my magic again?"

Blaze blinked in confusion; certain he hadn't heard Fable right. "You want me to teach you how to use your magic? Wouldn't it be better to ask an actual magic user for something like that? Like Gwydion, or even Eero?"

Fable shrugged, ducking his head self-consciously to his food. "You can say no if you don't want to do it."

"No, that's not it," Blaze rushed, reaching forward to take Fable's free hand, and force him to look up at him. He ignored the soft zing that went through him where their skin touched. Before realizing he'd overstepped, he dropped the connection, cheeks flaming more. "I just—they would be more qualified."

"Yeah, they probably would be," Fable agreed. "But you knew me then."

Blaze nodded dumbly. It was a stupid idea. Gwydion would know better than anyone how to do this, but he couldn't seem to stop himself from agreeing. The remainder of their dinner passed in companionable chitchat. They talked about movies, and patients, and anime. The words flowed freely between them as if they were old friends, and Blaze supposed maybe they finally were. When they were done, Blaze walked Fable to the door, a little smile tugging at his lips.

"You know," Fable said as he stopped right before the open door. "You're really sweet when you aren't snarling at people all the time." Then he moved onto his toes and pressed a lingering kiss to Blaze's cheek before turning to trot out into the hall. "I'll see you tomorrow for my lessons," he called over his shoulder as he scurried down the hall.

Blaze shut the door behind him, a deep blush settling into his cheeks.

"Don't screw this up, Blaze," Gwydion warned from where they had suddenly appeared beside the door. "You're getting a second chance at this, and if you screw it up, he will not give you another."

"I–I'm not — " Blaze stuttered, his hand lifting to press to the still tingling skin where Fable had kissed him.

"Not what?" Gwydion prompted.

"Not good enough for him. I never was." Blaze sighed, shoulders sagging. Gwydion smacked him upside the head, and Blaze glared at the witch. "What the hell was that for!"

"For thinking you get to make that decision for him. You let Fable decide who's good enough for him. That mage is tougher than you ever gave him credit for. He doesn't need you protecting him, not even from himself." Gwydion's golden eyes had narrowed, full lips pressed into a thin, severe line. "Understood?"

"Yes, Gwydion." Blaze rolled his eyes, ducking his head.

"Good. Now, go to your room. You've got studying to do. I've left some books of magic on your bedside table. I suggest you read them through before your lesson tomorrow with Fable."

<h1 style="text-align:center">THIRTEEN</h1>

Fable was nervous for his first magic lesson with Blaze. He remembered the subtle rush of power in a vague, distant way from when he'd been a mage. But that was all he had—a dusty old memory. *Will it be the same,* he wondered. And what would he use his magic for once he had use of it again? Gwydion seemed to throw their magic around like it was spare change, but Fable knew that mages didn't have that kind of power. The witch was, and would always be, more powerful than he was. Still, maybe he could use it to put some good out into the world.

After knocking, he bounced on his toes while he waited for Gwydion or Blaze to answer the door. What greeted him on the other side of the door was a tired-looking Blaze. The other man had bags beneath his brilliant amber eyes. He yawned into the back of his hand before stepping back to let Fable into the apartment.

"Is now not a good time?" Fable asked. "We can try again this weekend."

"No, it's all right. I just had a late night." Blaze stifled another yawn, shaking his head. "Lots of reading."

Fable nodded; his brow still raised high. He should leave. He should insist that they do this some other time. But he was too excited to wait any longer, and a selfish part of himself didn't want to put this off. "If you're sure," he whispered.

"I'm sure. Go sit, I'm just gonna grab some water." Blaze headed off to the kitchen without another word. He returned a moment later with two glasses of water and held one out to Fable.

"Is water part of it? Do I need to like—focus on the water or something?" Fable asked, squinting his eyes down at the clear liquid as he clutched the glass.

Blaze snorted, rolling his eyes. "No, Gwydion just always says it's rude to invite someone in and not at least give them a glass of water."

"I think you're supposed to offer it and ask if they want anything." Fable laughed softly, taking a sip from the glass.

Blaze scowled, his brows knitting. For a moment he looked like he wanted to yell at Fable for making fun of him. Then he closed his eyes, took a second, and nodded. "Yeah, I guess. But whatever," he said with an indifferent shrug.

"Thanks anyway." Fable took another sip and then set the glass down on the table in front of him. "So, where do we start?"

"From what I read," Blaze intoned, setting his own glass aside. "First, we have to tap into your magic before you can even use it. Which means finding it."

"Finding it? Where? Like in my pinky toe?"

Blaze grunted in annoyance. "No, like inside of you. You have to reach for it." Fable wasn't sure what Blaze meant by that, but he lifted his hand as if to reach out in front of him. "Not like that," Blaze grumbled, swatting his hand, drawing a nervous laugh from Fable. "It's like meditation. You close your eyes, you look inside, and you reach."

"Oh." Fable nodded. He still wasn't sure how to reach inside of himself, but he knew what meditation was, in theory anyway. He'd never done it, but it couldn't be that hard, could it?

"I'm not very good at the meditation thing. My therapist says it's not the tactic for me. But I know how to do it in theory," Blaze supplied.

"Therapist?" Fable asked, surprised. "You see a therapist?"

Blaze shrugged, ducking his head in embarrassment. "Yeah. But anyway," he pressed on, seeming to not want to talk more about this, and Fable let it drop for now. "You close your eyes and clear your mind as best you can. For many people it's hard, they can't seem to quiet down the thoughts."

"What do you do if that happens?" He would be one of those people, Fable just knew it. He'd dealt with a lot of insomnia throughout his life from the constant racing of an overactive brain. It was where the mumbling stemmed from too. How the hell was he supposed to quiet it down now so he could focus?

"She said you acknowledge the thought, give it a moment, and move on. There isn't really a way to make the thoughts stop coming, but by accepting them, you can keep them from taking over. So, let's try it?" Blaze suggested, a strange note of hope in his voice. "I mean, you're smart, you can do this."

That blind faith made Fable smile a little. He nodded, shutting his eyes and doing his best to clear his mind. It was no easy task, without the stimuli of his sight, the thoughts rushed him like small children did an ice cream truck. He clung to that metaphor, giving each of them their ice cream, and sending them on their way. Seconds ticked into minutes. Fable wasn't sure how long they sat there in silence, but Blaze remained still and waiting beside him—a true testament to the patience the dragon had learned.

Once all the children had gone, it was just Fable alone with himself. He listened to his breathing in the quiet of his mind, and then he heard it. Or maybe he felt it? Or maybe he saw it? He wasn't sure. But suddenly there was a warm, glowing green light at the forefront of his mind. It pulsed with a hum, warmth flooding from it into the rest of Fable's body, thrumming in his blood.

"You did it," Blaze's tone was soft and full of reverence. "Fable, open your eyes."

When Fable opened his eyes, he looked down at his hands to find them glowing softly with the same green light. A startled laugh left him. He looked up at Blaze, eyes wide with excitement. "It worked!" he squealed.

Blaze laughed, shaking his head. "Yeah, it did. I knew you could do it." There was pride in his voice as Blaze nodded to himself. It seemed the dragon had never had a doubt in his mind.

"What can I do with this?"

THE ANSWER WAS—NOT much. Although the supernatural were all around him—and more prevalent in New York than anywhere else—Fable was still surrounded by humans. Even if Fable had been as powerful as Gwydion— which he was not—he still had to keep humans from seeing him use his magic. Which, he realized, was the tricky part.

And it hit him hard when one of his patients had to be put down because of a tumor.

"Gwydion always says that people will believe what they want to," Eero argued from his position on the floor. "So, I don't see why you can't use your magic to heal all the animals who come to you at the vet."

"Because I work in an office full of humans. Not just humans, other veterinarians. They know the limits of our abilities as doctors for these animals. Even if I wanted to make every dog live to be fifty, so their human didn't have to be without them. Or rid every cat of cancer, I can't." Fable huffed, dejected as he sunk further down into the couch.

Blaze sighed, his hand lifting to rest on Fable's shoulder, rubbing a slow circle into it. It was a strange gesture, but Fable found comfort in it—warmth spreading through him. "No, you can't. But you can figure out other, smaller, things," Blaze insisted softly.

"Like easing their pain," Fable supplied softly, his hands wringing in his lap.

"Yes. And healing the ones you can," Blaze pressed, giving Fable's shoulder a little squeeze.

"Like Billy Bob's arthritis?" the words came out a little small, a little frail. It had been a little thing—infusing a little of his magic into the chewable tablets he usually prescribed to help with the pain of arthritis. Not enough magic to see that the dog would run around like a puppy again, but enough so he could go for short walks with his owners without pain. He could have done more, he wanted to do more. But there were rules. He had to be careful. And even still, that was more than he'd been able to do for Snickers.

"Yes, like Billy Bob's arthritis," Blaze agreed, a small amount of pride in his words. His big hand slipped from Fable's shoulder, and the mage did his best to ignore the feeling of cold skin left in the wake of a too-warm hand pressed there.

"Aura would understand," Eero argued. "You should tell her."

"Even if she did, she's not the only doctor in the office," Fable countered with a sigh.

Blaze's eyes narrowed on Eero. "You just want Fable to tell her so you can some out as fae. Don't be a selfish shit, Eero, it's not your neck on the line if you start another witch hunt," Blaze growled in warning.

Eero huffed but said no more on the subject.

AFTER WEEKS of testing his abilities, and practicing with books Gwydion had given him, Fable thought more and more about Blaze's predicament. Although Fable felt he had more or less tackled taming the dragon, Blaze still could not summon his fire in the way he once had.

"It's fine," Blaze insisted with a shrug. "I don't have any use for breathing fire anymore, anyway. What would I do? Go join the circus as a fire-eater?"

"No." Fable frowned. "But doesn't it feel like a part of you is missing?"

"Not really," Blaze muttered. But there was a hesitancy in his words, and his shoulders seemed to sag in on themselves.

"You'd think since you have control over your temper now you could control your fire again. That's what Gwydion said the curse was," Fable plowed on. He knew he was making Blaze a little uncomfortable with his insistence, but he couldn't seem to stop. After all, helping the dragon had been his mission before he'd died. And if he couldn't do that in this life, then all the other lives he'd lived had been in vain. Hadn't they? "I'll ask Gwydion about it."

"No," Blaze said firmly, a snarl on his lips. "Let it go, Fable. Worry about yourself for once." The tone was biting, and the words were unkind, but Fable didn't seem to notice. What he noticed was the pain lurking in the depths of those amber eyes.

"I just want to help you," Fable insisted, reaching for Blaze's hand to give it an encouraging squeeze.

"Well, I don't need your help. I didn't then, and I don't know." Blaze jerked his hand away. Despite the anger, Fable could still see the hurt.

IT LINGERED with Fable for days later. Drawing his attention away from everything around him as he pondered what that hurt could mean. He hated seeing Blaze hurting; he had to do something.

"Hello, Earth to Fable," Aura said, waving her hand in front of his face.

"Huh?" Fable blinked, eyes focusing again on his friend sitting across the table from him. "Oh, sorry."

"Where's your head at today? You've just been stirring your soup and not eating it for the last ten minutes." Aura sounded concerned. He hadn't meant to worry her, there was just so much going on.

He lifted a hand to scrub at his face, deciding he would probably regret this. "I need to tell you something, but it'll sound kind of crazy."

Aura shrugged. "I like crazy."

"Yeah, you do," Fable snorted, and then dove right in. He knew what it sounded like. He knew it was more fairy tale than reality, but he laid it all out for her. Explaining how he knew all of this to be true because he could remember vivid details that he shouldn't know. Like where exactly he'd lived in London, and how many children he'd had. He told her how he'd researched himself and found those names listed everywhere they ought to be. He told her about the dragon and how he'd always shown up. He lay all of his history out for his friend, hoping she wouldn't laugh in his face.

When he had finished, Aura sat in silence—a bit of bread she'd picked up to soak up some soup going soggy in her bowl where she'd dropped it. "That's a lot," she croaked.

"Uh, yeah, it is," Fable agreed, rubbing his sweaty palms on his pants legs. "So–um–yeah, that's the whole thing with me and Blaze."

Aura nodded slowly, as if considering the information, letting it roll around in her mind for a long moment. "And you're telling me all of this because?" she asked, and when Fable didn't immediately answer, she frowned. "It's not that I don't want to know what's going on with you and this guy, I do. But it sounded to me like he thought it'd be better if I didn't know. So, I'm just curious."

"Because he's hurting, and I don't know how to help him. Whenever I'm hurting, you always know what to say or do. I thought maybe you'd have some idea." Fable frowned deeply, pushing his now-cold soup away from him.

"Hmm..." Aura hummed thoughtfully.

They sat in silence for a long while, the ebb and flow of the café around them doing nothing to quill the racing thoughts that threatened to take over Fable's mind, and blot out everything else. What was Aura thinking? Would she tell him to just cut all ties? Would she decide Blaze was toxic for him? Would she not want anything to do with

Fable anymore after what he'd said? Would he have to leave the veterinary clinic?

"Warm up my soup," Aura ordered at length.

"What?" Fable blinked in confusion.

"Warm up my soup with your magic, and I'll give you advice."

More blinking.

"Go on, show me what you're workin' with." She smirked encouragingly, sliding the bowl closer to him.

"This is silly," he grumbled, lifting his hand to pass it over top of the bowl. His freckled fingers and the liquid in the bowl both glowed for a moment, a brilliant green color, then it melted away.

Aura slid it back to herself, tapping her finger to the surface of the soup to test the temperature. "Neat!" she giggled excitedly.

Fable rolled his eyes, unable to stop himself from laughing with her. "Yeah, neat. Now, what about your advice?"

She held up a finger and took a careful slurp from her spoon, murmuring happily. Then she set down the spoon, steepled her fingers, and fixed Fable with a look that said whatever wisdom she was about to impart should have been obvious. "He's still blaming himself for what happened to you."

"What? That's stupid," Fable snorted. "I told him I forgave him."

Aura rolled her eyes. "You know for someone who has hundreds of years of experience, you're pretty dense. Just because you forgive someone doesn't mean they always forgive themselves. He's still feeling guilty because he hurt you."

"So, what do I do about it?" Fable asked, shoulders sagging a little.

"I guess you just need to convince him to let it go."

"How?"

"Heck, if I know. He's your dragon, not mine." Aura shrugged, going back to her soup.

"He's not my dragon."

"Yeah, ok."

FABLE THOUGHT ABOUT IT—A lot—over the coming days. He couldn't get it out of his mind—the image of that pained expression in Blaze's eyes. He needed to do something about it. So, he invited the other man to his apartment for dinner, and then ordered take out. Because he wasn't trying to test the durability of a dragon's stomach.

"I could have cooked," Blaze argued, opening up his chopsticks. "And we could have done it at Gwydion's. We at least have a table to eat at."

"I have a table." Fable frowned, gesturing to the coffee table between them. It wasn't ideal, sharing a meal while they sat cross-legged on his floor, on either side of the too-short table, but Fable wanted the privacy that his apartment would provide.

"This—" Blaze tapped on the table with one long finger. "Is a coffee table. It is not for eating meals at."

Fable shrugged. "But at least Gwydion won't walk in on us with one of their dates."

Blaze considered this, and nodded. "Yeah, guess not."

"Honestly, I didn't want our date interrupted by—" An image of Gwydion with their hands knuckle deep in a fairy's obnoxiously pink hair flashed through his mind, and he frowned.

"Wait, this is a date?" Blaze asked, stopping with his chopsticks held halfway to his lips.

"I-er-yeah-no-maybe-I don't know," Fable stuttered and then huffed. "Not really. I mean, I just wanted to talk to you."

Blaze quirked a brow, slowly lowering a bite of rice and chicken back to the takeout container. There was a patient look on his features, one Fable hadn't seen until recently. "Then talk."

Fable nodded, swallowing roughly, and inhaling to steady the nerves he felt fluttering in his stomach. Where had those come from? "I need you to forgive yourself," he said lamely. It felt stupid coming from his lips, but it was important, so he forged on even when Blaze eyed him blandly. "For everything that happened. I know you still feel guilty, and I want you to forgive yourself for it."

"Why?" Blaze asked.

"Because if this—" Fable gestured between them. "Is going to work, you can't keep hurting yourself over our history. It's in the past. I forgave you, and now need to forgive yourself."

"And what is *this*, exactly?" Blaze's words came out painfully slow. As if he were afraid of what the real answer would be.

"Wh-what?" Fable lifted his head, confused and flustered by the question.

"What is this? What are we? What am I to you?" Blaze's tone remained calm, but there was a vulnerability to his expression Fable had never seen before. The dragon was scared.

Fable flushed so hotly he was sure it had spread all the

way to his toes. He hadn't realized where this conversation would head, but now he wished he'd been better prepared. "Well, I uh—" Maybe if he had been more prepared, he'd have known what to say, and how to say it. Maybe he would have realized that he'd inevitably stumble over his words, and reveal more than he ought. "What do you want it to be?" the words shook a little, but Fable forced them out.

"I want," Blaze said, moving onto his knees and leaning across the table. He moved slowly, giving Fable the time to back away if he wanted. But Fable didn't. He wanted to lean into it. He too rose onto his heels, and pressed their foreheads together. They met in the middle. A soft, lingering kiss that made Fable's toes curl. It felt natural, right. Like all of their lives had been heading towards this, and only this. Like this was the only reasonable outcome for the centuries of pain, and longing, and misunderstandings. Maybe it was. Maybe this was how it was always supposed to be. Fable wasn't sure, but he wanted to find out. "More of these," Blaze whispered, words a little husky as he pressed a shorter kiss to Fable's lips.

"Yeah, me too," Fable whispered, only half coherent from the kiss.

Blaze smiled softly.

"So, umm..." Fable licked his dry lips, forcing his eyes up from where they'd fixated on Blaze's soft smile, to meet his amber eyes. "What do you say? Can you forgive yourself?"

"If you let me spend the rest of our lives making that shit up to you, yeah, I guess I can."

"So, more dates?"

Blaze laughed, a deep musical sound that sent Fable's heart stuttering. "Yeah, more dates. But you aren't cooking, ever."

Fable laughed too, and shoved the other man back, before flopping onto his own bottom on the floor. "Jerk."

Blaze shrugged.

A companionable silence fell between them as they stole glances at one another over the takeout boxes. Little smiles lit each of their faces, each one making Fable flush a little more.

FOURTEEN

Something mean, and violent, that Blaze had lived with for centuries, had become so much worse in the time he'd spent with Fable. Not that Blaze blamed Fable for it, he didn't. He knew what the beast was—thanks to Phoebe, he'd been able to identify it—it was doubt, and fear, and self-loathing, taught to him through years of being hunted by the humans around him.

The beast had quieted during therapy, but finally fallen completely silent the moment their lips touched. It was as if everything suddenly made sense, and there was no room left for doubt. He enjoyed the silence that followed, not feeling the familiar uncomfortable niggle to fill it with words that said nothing, and meant less.

When they'd finished eating, Blaze moved silently from his side of the coffee table to sit beside Fable. They sat with their sides pressed together as they watched a movie that Blaze couldn't be bothered to pay attention to. It was so oddly domestic and peaceful; he didn't want the evening to end.

But it did—as all good things must. Fable followed him

to the door, and Blaze bent to kiss his lips gently. Fable was chewing on his lower lip when Blaze pulled back to meet his eyes. "Spit it out," he ordered gently.

With a huff that sounded like a cross between a laugh and a scoff, Fable rolled his eyes. "I was just wondering—will you ask Gwydion to lift your curse now? That's how Alrik said it works, Gwydion has to lift it."

Blaze thought about the words for a moment. He'd never asked Gwydion about lifting the curse, even when he knew that's how it worked. Truthfully, it had been because he still thought he had more work to do. He had felt that he wasn't entirely in control of himself, and so hadn't earned the right to his fire yet. Now, things were different. "Yeah, I think I will."

A blinding smile lit Fable's face at this. "So, next time I see you, you'll have your fire back." Excitement laced every word. No fear. No trepidation. Just honest eagerness. It was so earnest, and sincere, it made Blaze's heart clench.

"I will." He nodded firmly.

"See you tomorrow, then." Fable moved onto his toes and kissed him again, this one longer, and slower, and deeper, than any of the previous ones.

Blaze let himself sink into it. Let it leave him dizzy. And then he floated to the elevator to head home.

FOR THE FIRST time since the birth of the dragon, he was truly free. And it was all thanks to the mage who tamed him.

ACKNOWLEDGMENTS

First off, thank you—the reader—for reading Blaze and Fable's story. I hope you enjoyed their journey of self discovery, and maybe learned something about healing in the process.

Their story might be over, but this is not the last you have heard of Gwydion and their interesting curses. So, be on the look out for more from them.

Next, I'd like the think my small hoard of beta-readers. You guys gave some excellent insight, and I really appreciate the quick turn around that made this release possible!

And last but certainly not least, thank you to my small writing support group. Tiss, Elle, and Jasmine—without you there would be no Lou.

THE CURSE OF FLOUR & FEELING

LOU WILHAM

Preview

PROLOGUE

Not so long ago—in a great city which you may or may not be familiar with known as New York—there lived a young girl by the name of Darcie Gyeong Alston named so for her dark hair, dark eyes, and her mother's family name Gyeong. The Gyeongs were bakers, had been bakers for generations in Korea, and Gyeong Eun in spite of having never known another home outside of New York, was no different. Thus Darcie was raised, as baker's children so often are, like dough. In a warm kitchen, freckled with flour, and sweetened by sugar. And it was understood, always, that one day she would be a baker herself.

A few short blocks away—a world away by New York standards—there lived a child named Atsushi Haruki, but from a young age zir friends just called zir Hari. Hari was bright, and charming, and clever. The kind of child who drew everyone into zir orbit. The kind of child who never had trouble making friends. With a creative spirit, and a quick mind, ze saw potential everywhere ze looked.

ABOUT THE AUTHOR

Born and raised in a small town near the Chesapeake Bay, Lou Wilham grew up on a steady diet of fiction, arts and crafts, and Old Bay. After years of absorbing everything, there was to absorb of fiction, fantasy, and sci-fi she was left with a serious creative habit that just won't quit. These days, she spends much of her time writing, drawing, and chasing a very short Basset Hound named Sherlock.

When not, daydreaming up new characters to write and draw she can be found crocheting, making cute bookmarks, and binge-watching whatever happens to catch her eye.

Learn more about Lou and her future projects on her website: http://louinprogress.net or join her mailing list at: http://subscribepage.com/mailermailer

Die From A Broken Heart by Elle Beaumont

Abigail's relationship with her boyfriend, Seth, is teetering on the edge of self-destruction. The recent lack of communication and cold shoulder has become unbearable. So, when Seth's ghost hunting job takes him on a trip to South Carolina, Abigail decides to join, and use the down time to hopefully rekindle their flame.

When they arrive at the historical antebellum house—which is allegedly haunted—Abigail quickly learns there is more to it than meets the eye, and within the walls there is a dark story, and presence, threatening to pull her under, especially when a mysterious stranger shows up.

If Abigail can't find a way to survive the eerie house, then she may have more to worry about than the possibility of a broken heart

Add to your TBR
Available Now

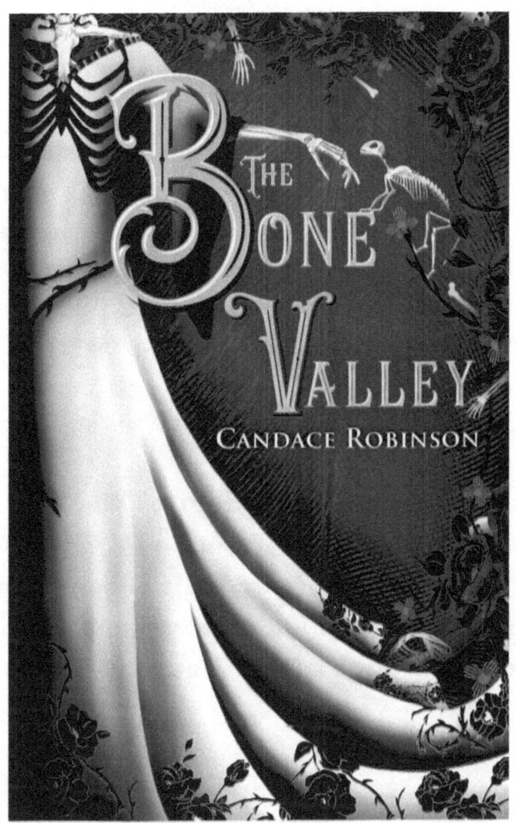

The Bone Valley by Candace Robinson

An unexpected and addictive NA Stand-Alone Fantasy Romance.

He's a lover. She's a thief. A magic like no other will bind them together.

After the death of his parents, Anton Bereza works hard to provide for his younger siblings. Love has never been in the cards for him, especially after desperation forces Anton to sell himself for coin. And he has no idea that, beneath the city of Kedaf, lies a place called the Bone Valley.

When Anton's jealous client plots against him, he is cursed to spend eternity in a world where all that remains are broken bones. There, Anton meets Nahli Yan—a spirited woman who once tried to steal from him—and his cards begin to change. But as the spark between them ignites, so does their desire to escape. All that stands in their way is the deceitful Queen of the Dead, who is determined to wield her vicious magic to break Anton and Nahli apart. Forever.

Perfect for fans of Kingdom of the Wicked, A Court of Thorns and Roses, and Daughter of Smoke & Bone. The Bone Valley is one delicious romantic fantasy filled with swoon, enemies to lovers, and unique magic that you won't want to miss!

Add to your TBR
Available Now

Constellations of Scars by Melissa Eskue Ousley

Not all gifts are a blessing. Some are a curse.

When Amelia turned 12, she began growing pearls. Every month, a crop of beautiful pearls bursts from the skin on her back. Her mother, Denise, believes her daughter is blessed, and sells the pearls to put food on the table. Amelia sees her condition as a curse. As the pearls form, her body aches and her skin grows feverish. The harvest of pearls brings temporary relief from the pain, but leaves her back marred by scars. Denise hides Amelia away from the world, worried that Amelia's gift will be discovered and she will be abducted for the wealth she can provide. Now a young woman, Amelia realizes she has become her mother's captive, and plans her escape. When she runs away from home, she finds a new family in a troupe of performers at a museum of human oddities. She soon discovers the world is much more dangerous than her mother feared.

Add to your TBR
Available Now